A SIN TO KNOW

TERENCE PATRICK HUGHES

Praise for Terence Patrick Hughes

"Terence Patrick Hughes' writing is delightfully detailed yet familiar, his characters seemingly stolen from my childhood adventures on the other side of the train tracks. I can't wait to see what he does next."

— **J.B. MARLOW**, Editor, *Rock Salt Journal*

"Terence Hughes is a writer who seamlessly blends humor, tension, and social critique. His is a voice that is both satirical and deeply observant of the world around him. His prose crackles with energy and a knack for capturing the absurdities of everyday life, showing the reader how even the ordinary can unravel into sharp revelations, uncomfortable truths, and unexpected hilarity."

— **MATTHEW JOHNSON**, Editor, *Portrait of New England*

"Terence Patrick Hughes has a knack for hilarity and heart in his writing. We love him."

— **KIERAN COTTRELL**, General Editor, *Egg + Frog*

Praise for *A Sin to Know*

"Brutally tense and wickedly funny, A Sin to Know is a breathless page-turner that cuts deep, lingers in the bones, and haunts the tender-hearted with a question: How far would we go for all the flawed humans we love?"

SOFIE JUSTICE Author of *The Other Farmhouse* Editor-in-Chief, *Press Pause Press*

ISBN: 979-8-2746-8178-0
Imprint: Independently published
Published by Yes Let's Go Productions
Lake Hill, New York

Cover design by B & D Studio
Printed in the United States of America

For my one-of-a kind wife and two-of-a-kind kids

"Read books and drink water."

"Knowledge forbidden? Suspicious, reasonless.
Why should their Lord envy them that?
Can it be a sin to know? Can it be death?"

JOHN MILTON, *PARADISE LOST*, BOOK IV

Chapter One

The kid got hit on the bridge, my first guess is a sedan or jeep, traveling fast enough to knock him ten feet in the air and tumbling another twenty down the embankment to the creek's edge. A few inches of early spring snow covered him up for more than a day, but even after the melt you could see by the streaked remains of blood on the ice that the boy had tried to crawl for his life back up to the road. Besides the freezing temperature, his progress was checked by two broken legs, a collapsed lung, and a massive gash to the head, but he had been alive for several hours after the accident, maybe longer. As for the driver, by the looks of what was left of their boot prints in the snow and mud, they got out, examined the tragic scene from several angles on the bridge, then got back in the car and peeled away.

My cell rang a little after 5 AM.

"You pick now to call?" I mumbled into the phone, my other hand reaching over to the empty side of the bed.

"Sheriff, it's Sam at the diner."

I sat up right away—no one calls this early just to say good morning. "Awright, let me have it."

"Well, I got these guys here…said they found a body. I mean, their dog did." His voice lowering into a gravelly whisper. "Said they were hunting foxes but sumbitches look like duck poachers to me."

"Hold on to em'. I'll be right there."

The house was cold and dark. I crawled back into the uniform that I'd discarded only a few hours earlier and stumbled downstairs. In better days, Tammy would've gotten up with me and started coffee before I could even get my belt and gun out of the lockbox. She had this way of whispering not to wake Cliff so that we might enjoy a few moments alone, talking in the kitchen or having some fun on the sofa. Nowadays, any talk is curt and the fun has gone away like a packed-up circus that never broke even and won't ever return to these parts again. A sad last act to the greatest show on earth.

Once I was out into the chilly, still dark morning, I let the truck warm up while I dialed up the night operator at the station.

She sounded fresh for the hour, no doubt from that nasty instant coffee of hers. "Rock Hollow Sheriff's Office. Stacey speaking."

"You don't need to say all that when it's me."

"I know." Her tone turned serious. "You're up early. Can't be good. Listen, Mariel Hinckle called 'bout a half hour ago, said her youngest, Billy, never been home since night before last. Cause it's school vacation she thought he was stayin' over at—"

"Shit," I spat and pulled the truck down the long, bumpy driveway and out into the street. "What do I always say? Call me the second it comes in."

"I'm sorry. I figured I'd let you sleep a little, you was here so late with that B&E."

"Anyway. I'm on it, if she calls back, tell her I'll get over there soon as I can."

"OK, Sheriff. I am sorry. I just figured with Tammy taken off again, I'd let you—"

I hung up and tossed the phone on the passenger seat. The problem with good employees is that they know all the boss's shit. My mother-in-law lives about two hours north, deep wilderness for a shallow woman, and without a word Tammy often disappears to 'mamas' for a week or sometimes longer, usually after one of our drop-down fights. Our bouts never come close to physical abuse but boy can we shred each other emotionally. A couple of years ago, she started seeing someone up there, telling me with flat-out honesty, like she had picked up woodworking.

"I've started with somebody," is how she put it, with her always pretty face twisted into a bizarre look of hurt and triumph.

So, I soon took up woodworking myself. Like a million other marriages, we held it together for the kid, but this week she played dirty pool and took Cliff with her, even though he and I had plans for my day off to go check out a used riding mower for sale over in Hookfield and then get some steaks. There's no telling how long he resisted her tireless begging before leaving me a scribbled note that said '*Sorry Dad*' on the kitchen table. Yeh, me too. I imagined him sitting around all last night with that angry vulture of a grandmother spewing all kinds of shit about me, while her daughter went out to practice serial adultery.

"God-damned," I whispered and flicked on the overhead flashers, speeding through red lights and stop signs that have no meaning until folks woke up. An empty town tells no tales.

After collecting the men and their dog from the diner, they led me to the scene, then I let them continue to their hunt with a reminder that foxes do not fly or say 'quack'. They had been smart not to mess with the body, leaving only the dog's prints visible on the slope, soon joined by my own as I took some photos with my phone of the impact and landing spots and the markings from the kid's last slow crawl to his death.

I'd seen the boy around—a few years younger than Cliff, one of many faces in the crowd of sort-of-well behaved teenagers within my jurisdiction. I stood for a long time near the body as hot anger brewed inside, but I fought it off by finishing my job up on the bridge, capturing some half-decent tire prints and texting them along with the other images to the state police. Finally, I called to wake up our local grim reaper.

"Hello?" Daniel Miller croaked after picking up on the seventh ring.

"Hey, it's Blake. Sorry, Dan," I was whispering and didn't know why. "We got a local teen out by Hopkins Creek Bridge. Hit-and-run."

"Oh, my," Daniel gasped through a yawn and groaned as he

got himself going. "Are you helping?"

"Can't. Gotta go break it to the family. Soon as you get here."

We exchanged our usual business bullshit and hung up. Daniel is a strange loner of a man who operates the only funeral parlor for forty miles around. Due to a sharp mind and familiarity with the dead, he's our default choice to serve as a local coroner. He'll transport the body back to the parlor where it'd have to sit on ice until the staties can get their ass down here to make the case official. Hopefully in twenty-four hours but likely longer. An upside to two-bit law enforcement is that it's rarely eventful, but when something bad does happen, the slow-moving gears can make life feel like its stuck on hold to the beat of some bad elevator Muzak.

After twenty minutes or so of wishing that I still smoked cigarettes, I heard the distinct rumble of Daniel's minivan. The moment that he turned the corner; he waved and gave a strange smile with the odd demeanor of one who profits from the dead. As he pulled up near me, we both leaned out of our windows and Daniel turned down the soft-rock music blaring on the stereo.

"He's over on the slope. Not a pretty sight," I said.

"Never are," Daniel remarked, shrugging his shoulders. "Any idea who did it?"

"Not yet," I replied, kicking my truck into gear.

"Might be some paint on the clothing. I'll let you know. How's the family?"

"Oh, same as always," I deadpanned. "Another day, another holler."

We shared a brief chuckle, which broke off quickly as we fell back into the matter at hand, and I left him to his work.

The visit with Mariel Hinckle went as badly as expected. When I arrived at her house, she took one look at my sad face and burst into hysterics. There were two of her grown kids hanging around, and they tried their best to console her until I poured a big drink from a bottle of cheap vodka lying in the freezer. After three good belts, she managed to sit with me alone on her back porch. The weak morning sun was losing its initial battle with the chilly air, and even though Mariel only had on a blouse, jeans, and socks, she didn't shiver once.

We knew each other somewhat, because Mariel's husband is away in the army seemingly forever, which has spurred Mariel to drop the Adams from her surname, Tammy's had her over for dinner a bunch of times. She's older than my wife by about a decade, but she sure doesn't act like it or look like it for that matter. Those evenings would wind up with the three of us blasting Van Halen records and dancing around the living room.

"We gotta find the fucker that did this," she kept repeating, squeezing hard on a fistful of tissues.

"We will," I replied, bumping my shoulder lightly to hers for assurance. "Staties'll help."

Once I'd gently explained that she had to go over to the funeral home and identify the body, I tried to calm her by detailing how a lot of hit-and-runners get caught and this one would do big jail time. She just needed to lie low and let law enforcement do their jobs.

She sat up straight and stiff. "No. I don't want 'em locked up. I'm callin' my brothers."

As sassy and pretty as Mariel Hinckle turned out to be, her brothers are an entirely different story. Before passing away, the old sheriff who hired me recounted many tales of having to chase down and lock up the "Hinckle turds" for everything from harassment and public drunkenness to larceny and assault. Growing up, whenever the eldest brother Ben's pickup came roaring down the street, all the kids would scatter as if the devil himself was behind the wheel.

By the time I started as a deputy, Ben had moved down to New Jersey to set up some kind of business, certainly illegal, and the two others, middle brother, Dicky, and the youngest, Derrick, followed soon after. After becoming sheriff, I only had a run-in with Ben. He owned a hundred-acre parcel of woodland off the bypass that rumor said he'd won in a card game, another rumor being that he'd cheated like hell. Nearing about a Hinckle-free year on the job, complaints started coming in about dump trucks full of debris pulling into Ben's lot. Sure enough, I found a crudely dug pit overflowing with gravel, concrete, scrap metal and lumber and a closer inspection turned up a couple of rusted oil tanks. Instead of reporting him to the environmental protection cops, I tracked down Ben myself and told him to clean up the illegal dump or expect the state to be in touch with a sizable lawsuit. Let's just say that Ben did not appreciate my gesture because the next industrial-waste laden dump truck that pulled into town also carried a couple of guys that looked like extras from a mafia movie. Those were the days when I still hung at *The Deuces Wild* and, unfortunately for them, the two thugs tracked me down while my boys and I were tying one on. By the time we carried the wannabe mobsters out of the bar and tossed them both into the back of the dump truck, they looked more like palooka boxers after brutal TKOs.

I got one more rage-filled phone call from Ben, promising to bring down all kinds of hell on my head, but a local realtor told me later that he helped Ben sell the property back to the man who'd lost the card game, a nice old guy named Darnold who's since passed away. Of course, Ben made a profit on the whole venture and has failed to deliver on his promise of destroying my life, until possibly today.

"Listen, Mariel," I said, preparing to warn her off any vigilante justice, "I'm not about to put up with—"

"They killed my baby," she hissed, shutting me right up. "What would you do if it was your kid, huh? Sit around and go fuckin' crazy?"

"You know how much—"

"So help me if you don't catch em fast…" She stood up and pushed open the door, but before disappearing inside she added quietly, "Thanks for coming by, Blake."

As I walked to the car, Mariel's sobbing wails started up again inside the house. Through a window I caught sight of her shuddering body in an armchair, flanked by the consoling family members. For a moment, I imagined that if I had married her instead of Tammy, then none of this would have happened. Then just as quickly, I shook the idea off. When you get way too personal about the job, it lands you in deep trouble every time.

I spent the rest of the morning checking out surrounding town garages and auto repair shops up and down the bypass. No recent collisions to report but each mechanic promised to look out for a banged-up front passenger section that would probably be explained away as a deer hit. Next, I swept a few miles on the road to and from the bridge in case any wheel damage might've forced the culprit to dump the vehicle in the woods.

While I was driving, the state police came back to me and said they'd have two patrolmen at my disposal but due to resource shortages, best case will be within twenty-four hours or possibly forty-eight, which meant zero backup while dealing with Mariel's brothers' harsh brand of Sunday services. The smartest thing would've been to call up Frank Sweeney and his son who occasionally perform as deputies but Frank drinks like a fish and is useless on weekends while his son is an ornery little bastard and would likely sign on with the posse as soon as he caught a whiff of blood.

Adding a burr of annoyance to the circumstances, when the staties rang I thought it might be Cliff calling to crawl back into my good graces, but the phlegmy grumble belonged to a short-tempered dispatcher named Frank. By the time I hung up with Mr. Personality and got back into town, the afternoon was already in full swing. At the station house, which used to be an old laundromat and still looks like it on the outside, I checked in with Barbara, my day operator. Barbara's a long-married wife and mom pushing fifty who is a bit talkative, but outside of her job she does nothing but read books, eat baked goods, and drink whiskey and I admire her on all counts. After a greeting and a brief update on her sick guinea pig, she got down to business.

"We just got one call about a downed tree up on Overlook Drive, but I guess Billy Wettles—the dad and not the kid, who is a piece of work, let me tell you, anyway old Billy already diced it up with a chainsaw." Barbara then got to what she wanted to start off with in the first place. "Any leads on the poor kid out at the creek bridge?"

"Can't talk about it right now," I snapped and headed for the door, calling back in consolation as I was almost gone, "but I'll catch you up soon enough."

I decided to head down Main Street and stop over at the tavern, exchanging curt greetings on the way with a couple of folks on the sidewalk, who had just as many questions about the hit-and-run as Barabara, but far less manners. Pulling open *The Deuces'* heavy wood door with the big brass handle always fills me with a rush of good and familiar expectations, like going back for the hundredth time to an old friend's house, albeit one I used to crawl home from. The sunlight dappling through the grime of the big front window, mixed with the minimal lighting inside, gave an odd glow to the few folks seated at tables, enjoying liquid lunches.

Of course, Elmore the early bird was anchoring the bar.

"Greetings, Marshall!" he crowed upon catching sight of me.

Elmore is on the shorter side, but his stocky build and outsized personality place him at the center of the action wherever he goes. He used to teach many things at many colleges up and down the East Coast until he could no longer outrun his indiscriminate dalliances with the bottle and various undergraduates. Now, he does a couple of virtual lectures a week, and the local joke is that he finally doesn't have to wait until after class to take his pants off.

I grinned and rested my palms on the bar. "Hey, El. Gettin' a head start?"

Elmore raised his glass of bourbon. "'Come what may, all bad fortune is to be conquered by endurance."

He knocked the drink back, placed the glass on the bar, and tipped toward me on his stool.

"That's Virgil. Do you know he may have predicted the birth of Jesus Christ? Screw the Aeneid. The clairvoyant son-of-a-bitch should've spent his time laying down bets at the chariot races."

"Hey, Sheriff," bellowed Mickey, a tall young man just

beginning to put on mid-to-late-twenties weight, as he came out from the supply room behind the bar, "long time no see."

"Yup, been survivin' on milk and cookies."

"Poor man," Elmore lamented.

"Wanna Coke?" Mickey offered, reaching below to the fridge.

"Nah," I sighed because I wanted something way stronger than that, "but I gotta ask you some questions."

"Oh…OK."

"Shall I sequester myself during the interrogation?" Elmore inquired. "If so, please pour me a double, Mikhail."

I waved Elmore to keep his seat. "S'pose you'll hear soon enough. Had a hit-and-run. Mariel Hinckle's kid's dead."

Mickey winced.

"The little one?"

"Yup." I glanced over at the tables and then back at Mickey. "She's all broke up. Gonna have my hands full with a lynch mob of her brothers tomorrow."

"The teardrops of fascism," Elmore added.

"First off, anybody been kickin' it up more than usual the night before last?"

"I mean…we got happy hour on Thursdays. Place is always packed…" Mickey let his words drag as he looked down at his feet.

"Remember, Mickey," I spoke slow, putting severity into my tone. "You tell me stuff, and that's always the end of it."

"Well…I guess Keith Griffin was pretty messed up." Mickey admitted before quickly covering his tracks. "I didn't serve him nothin' but beer, and only a couple. He was shit-faced when he got here. Startin' trouble with everybody."

"Happen to know what he was drivin'?"

"N-no. I didn't give em more than two beers, Sheriff." He was starting to stammer.

A patron at the tables called Mickey over, and he was glad for it. I had no problem with his anxiety. A big part of running the only tavern in a small town is managing trouble without losing customers.

"You be good, El," I nodded and turned to go.

"There's no mystery to it."

I turned back to him but didn't answer right away. The reflection in the mirrored wall behind the bar caught my attention. My features looked the same, excepting my shadowed face was hollowed with fatigue, but everything else—the backs of the bottle rows, the lights strung from the ceiling above our heads, the people knocking back drinks at their tables—looked so much better on the other side of the glass than out here.

"Huh?"

"The hit-and-run…" Elmore raised his wiry, gray eyebrows. "Particularly in a fatal case. We live in a society obsessed with discipline and punishment; in such matters, one is essentially guilty upon impact. As for the human condition, when faced with such instant and severe circumstances, flight is logical. One could reason it an overpowering nervous impulse."

"You're saying it's OK to…" I didn't want to stick around, particularly to tussle with an overweight, over-educated drunk, but my nerves were jumping.

"I pass no judgment. My point is that every last human being is treacherously weak to begin with, and when plunged into seconds of terror, the mind will command one thing even whilst the heart demands another. It's only afterwards that the ethical questions begin their haunting harangue." Elmore turned to call Mickey back to the bar. "What in the name of bloody Bacchus is taking so long?"

I rested a hand on his back.

"I appreciate your smarts, El. But you smash into a boy and leave him to bleed and die in the freezing cold—then you got no ethics, plain and simple, and you deserve to go in the same way…or worse."

"Spoken like a soldier of justice."

I gave him a harsh look followed by a wink, satisfying myself with the thought that you can read every book in the world and still not know shit about people.

On the way out, Mickey caught up with me at the door.

"Don't tell him I said he was wrecked." His concerned whisper showed that, like many men in town, he was terrified of pissing off Keith Griffin.

"Deal," I assured him and left with Elmore's sing-song farewell following me out.

"Until we meet again, Marshall!"

I went across the street to grab a turkey sandwich at the meat store. Although my first meal of the day is always a hasty affair, this one lasted about thirty seconds and I hardly tasted a bite of it on the ride over to Griffin's place. Keith is a few years younger than me and, although we played some football together and went to the same parties, we weren't friends back in school. Long after graduation, we got paired up during a bass tournament, and that one afternoon in a boat in the middle of Echo Lake catching fish and crushing beers turned us into decade-long drinking buddies. Any time I got the itch to raise hell, which happened a lot after Tammy and I quit trying to be husband and wife, I called Keith and woke up a day later looking like a rat drowned in a rum barrel. Only he was a violently miserable drunk and extricating him from all the many episodes of social mayhem and drop-down brawls became truly exhausting.

Then came a Friday night house party that went on for two days, where I woke up on the front porch and stumbled into my living room to find Keith and Tammy on the couch locking tongues and pawing at each other. The drop-down brawl that ensued lasted a good five minutes and cost me close to two grand in busted furniture and glassware, not to mention a visit to the doctor for stitches, after throwing Keith through the screen door where he finally got knocked out cold, slamming his ugly head into a porch beam.

After letting him rot in a jail cell for most of Sunday, I let him go with a dire warning that I'd kill them both if he ever came near Tammy again, a promise repeated to my wife in regrettable anger. Not sure if we were ever the same again after that. Most marriages suffer when one spouse threatens to murder the other, but we kept our heads down and trooped onward. I cut Keith out of my life like a festering boil, only seeing him on the occasion of locking him up for his own safety, always a mighty task and once even requiring a taser.

Many folks around town followed my lead shunning Keith, which made him act even crazier, for the attention I suppose, until he had to do a long stretch in prison for assault after a bar fight on the coast when he nearly killed a guy who had offered to buy his girlfriend a drink. She smartly ran out on him while he was incarcerated, as did a series of girls after he got out. Maybe he would've turned things around if we'd stayed friends. More than goddamn likely not.

Keith lives about fifteen miles out of town near the old paper mill, a massive, crumbling edifice of red brick and receding mortar that at one time employed over a thousand hands. His house is near the edge of the woods, a hundred yards from the mill, and is the last standing structure of an abandoned worker village. Although it only consists of three rooms that Keith heats by burning wood, cut illegally, and illuminates with battery-powered lanterns, it manages in its rustic simplicity and rural isolation to be more cottage than shack, if you don't mind busted snowplows and engine blocks as lawn ornaments or conducting one's private business in an outhouse.

Keith's two pickups were parked to the side of the house, and one of them had his carpentry tools in the back. As I got out of my truck and moved to the covered porch, he pulled open the front door and stepped out, first zipping up his orange puffer and then plopping himself down on a canvas camping chair. His cheeks were flushed from working outside and a soiled mesh baseball cap was cocked back on top of his long, greasy sandy-brown hair.

"You're early, Sheriff. I ain't even robbed the bank yet," he said and took a long sip from the bottle of beer in his hand.

"Glad to almost bust you," I chuckled but he couldn't miss the fire in my eyes. Get shit-faced enough times with a man, and he catches a glimpse of your soul. "I gotta ask you some questions."

Keith set his shoulders and took a long look at me. I stared back at his booze and weather-ravaged face. It still hung on to a bit of that devil's youth.

"So?"

"Mariel Hinckle's kid got hit by a car. Dead. Driver took off."

"And you come here?"

"Listen, Keith." I put a foot up on the good front step, the other two were rotting out. "I got other people to talk to, so…"

"Woo-eee, I'm first in line." Keith jumped up and I tensed, ready for trouble, but he headed into the house.

"Where you goin'?"

He stopped just over the threshold inside with his back to me, one hand gripping the door.

"To get a beer. Want one?"

"No thanks."

"Good, cause you weren't gettin' it, asshole."

He left the door wide open and seconds started to pile up. Because I'd been in a couple of hairy situations serving warrants to mountain people, I unsnapped my holster and put a porch post between the door and myself.

"Keith?" He'd been gone over a minute, and I wasn't going to allow him any longer. "Keith, get outta that house!"

The crack of a twist-off cap opening was enough to make my hand tremble, but I drifted nearer to the steps as he came out holding his beer up high.

"Just openin' up a new case, Sheriff," he scoffed and re-took his seat. "You gettin' skittish in your old age?"

"You were out Thursday night, right?"

"Plenty of witnesses to that." Keith drew back his cap by the brim and then popped a cigarette into his mouth, lighting it from a box of matches on the wicker table by his side. "Can't say that I remember any of them, though."

"A kid's dead, Keith."

"Heard you." He took a long drag and blew it out through his nose.

"I'm gonna look around," I muttered and stepped toward the side of the house where he parked his vehicles.

"Used to be a day…" Keith hollered after me.

The first thing I did was examine the ground, but the wet air from the nearby river had done its job and made it a mess of snow and mud, impossible to pick out one tire track from the next. The two pickups were parked together, the first an ancient rusted-black Ford that stood with its hood open and half the motor-parts missing. I glanced at its passenger side anyway, which was in real rough shape but not the kind of damage I was looking for. The other one was the old Chevy that he drives regularly, beat up but still sturdy. The hood and sides were scratched and dented plenty, but not in the right location to mark it as a killing machine.

"See them gouges under the side mirror?" Keith appeared from behind me while I looked over the Chevy. "Got swiped good playing a round of chicken with the boys. And this one…"

He walked around my side and rubbed the badly dented fender.

"Got this one when I bet Hank Denning I could kill a cow without a gun. I lost."

After taking a last drag of the cigarette and casting it aside, he came right up to me and didn't blow the smoke into my face but close enough.

"Hell, a few of these dings and scratches are from nights out with you, Sheriff." He then gritted his teeth hard. "I banged her up plenty over time, sure. But I didn't kill no fuckin' kid."

"Where's your jeep?" I shot back.

"Sold it."

"When?"

He backed off and headed toward the house.

"I don't know. Couple weeks ago."

"To who?"

I started right after him and he slowed.

"You heard me! To who?"'

He whirled around. I was bigger than him, but he always had a way of surprising his opponents. I took a step back and was embarrassed enough that I purposefully put a hand to his chest, which he slapped away.

"Easy, Keith."

"You piece a shit. Why don't you take off that holster and badge and we make this visit unofficial?"

"You gonna answer my question?"

We locked eyes and neither of us flinched for some moments that were so quiet I could hear the rush of the river in the distance.

"Look at you," Keith smirked, but his breath was coming hard. "Real big man. How's it feel tryin' so hard to be the good guy all the time?"

"I wouldn't know."

"Bullshit." Keith grimaced and shook his head. "You used to be bad enough to hang with the likes of me. Then you climbed up on your horse and put on the white hat. That's you, asshole. The Lone Ranger. A lawman hidin' behind a mask."

"Who'd you sell it to?"

"Stop fuckin' with me! You already got the whole town treatin' me like a scumbag just cause I felt up your wife—"

"Shut your mouth about her! I told you…"

"And now you want to pin a fuckin murder on me? Go get your warrant, Lone Ranger. I ain't answerin' any more of your sneaky-ass questions. Get the hell out of here. Get out!"

Keith jumped over the steps and onto the porch. I stood and watched him chug the rest of the beer and then smash the empty bottle on the floorboards.

"You're trespassin' now. It's my right to put a few shots in the air. Never can tell where the bullets land after that. Maybe in your fat fuckin' pussy ass."

I took a few steps toward him. The cauldron inside me was bubbling and I was ready. I swear, I was ready. Thankfully, a better plan came together in my mind. I spat on the ground, marched back to the truck, got inside, and pulled out with fury.

I smacked the dashboard hard as livid chatter filled my head.

He wants a warrant, then I'll get one from the judge. If he ain't around, tough shit. I'm locking that motherfucker up on suspicion until the staties get here. Sold his jeep. Bullshit! I'll get Conner Nason to dredge the pond behind the house. I bet he did it, the rotten son-of-a-bitch! Maybe let Mariel's brothers visit him in the cell for a few minutes, tell em they got to stop just short of killing him.

Only after that last evil notion did I retrieve some sense, reminding myself of the differences between me and the goons in a posse. This job was not supposed to lead to a lower place in life, damn it, and unless I follow the law, I'm not worthy of the badge.

I switched on the radio and let a John Denver song calm me down, but I was still so pissed off that I stopped at Judge Anderson's house, anyway. He'd just returned from a round of early-season golf and still had on a ridiculous pair of checkered pants. His wife wore a similar outfit but paired it with a much deeper scowl on her face. The judge made it clear that he despises pop-ins and recommended that I spend my time tracking down other leads but also promised to approve a warrant on Monday.

"Let the state police get into a shootout with that nutcase," he grumbled before hastily showing me to the door.

For the last few hours of daylight, I drove around town inspecting driveways for suspect vehicles, cars parked out of sight or covered with tarps, but nothing turned up. Every time I pushed Keith Griffin out of my mind, he slithered back in with his ugly smirk and asshole attitude. I could see him standing up on that bridge, knowing full well that he'd hit somebody, either too drunk to reason or so lacking in human compassion that he fled. Well, if a mountain of bad karma was finally about to crumble over onto that son-of-a-bitch, then I'm going to do whatever is necessary to make it happen fast.

When I stopped at the station, Barbara had not yet been relieved by Stacey and was busy getting crumbs all over a magazine.

"Hi-ya, Sheriff," she said through a full mouth of oatmeal

raisin cookie. "You been out all day."

A paper plate piled with home-baked treats sat on the desk by her elbow. She and her kids are always baking goodies on Friday nights. Hordes of them end up at the station on Saturdays for her to pick at during the shift. They aren't bad cookies, but the family's recipe calls for so much sugar that they make my teeth ache.

"Not by choice, Barb. Believe me."

"So, what about that hit-and-run?" She flipped a page of the magazine and popped the last nibble into her mouth with one motion. "Any leads?"

"Yup." I moved over to the kitchenette to pour some lukewarm coffee into a paper cup, "I got a dispatcher who's suspiciously obsessed with the case. Making me wonder…"

"You know I just care about poor Mariel." Barbara's face took on a sad pout. "As a mother, it just kills me."

"It's a tragedy for sure." I took a big sip of the brackish day-old brew and set the cup down. "But talking about it instead of looking into it does me no good."

"Just kills me…" Barbara shook her head while snatching another cookie from the pile.

"Her brothers will be here tomorrow."

Barbara stopped chewing and shifted her widening eyes to me.

"Those shit-bums are trouble," she moaned.

"Can't tell them not to console their family," I said before collecting the house keys from my desk. "No law against it."

She eyed me as if I were playing dumb. "That ain't why they're coming."

"Once again we come to the power of action instead of just talk."

"What are you gonna do?" she shot right back.

"I'm not going to talk about it."

All of a sudden, I was starving but not enough to take on a night's worth of tooth pain for one of Barbara's sugar-bombs. For the life of me, I couldn't imagine what was in the fridge at home, but grabbing a meal out someplace required seeing people and I'd honestly had more than enough for one day.

"Night, Barb." I patted her on the shoulder on the way past. "Say hi to Stacey when she gets in."

"Will do." Barbara kicked back into her warm self. "Don't let the bedbugs bite!"

A nice trim of fading silver rested on the horizon as I bounced up my long, choppy driveway to the house, promising myself to get to those potholes next week. When I got closer, any dark, lingering thoughts of Keith Griffin shot out of my mind at the lively sight of the house lights blazing inside and the propane tank in the backyard giving off its low hum. Probably needs a new regulator. Another thing on the list to fix when I get the time.

I eased up behind Tammy's old Subaru, got out, and stepped up the brick walkway, briefly imagining us all apologizing and then hugging and making lots of food. Maybe even a drink or two, and then a full night of good sleep next to my wife's warm body. By the time I got to the door, the imagined aromas of microwaved leftovers and wishful snuggles had vanished. I was dead tired, and if these two wanted to battle me like a newly formed alliance looking to show off their power, then I would kill them with kindness, grab a sleeping bag, and go crash in the truck.

When I stepped into the house, the glow of the TV in the darkened den caught my eye, and there was Cliff sitting on a hassock right in front of the screen but not watching it. He was slouched over his phone, the images sending flickers of light dancing across his white T-shirt. My first impression was that he was really filling out into a muscular physique, but the lack of greeting got me pissed off all over again.

"How 'bout a hello?" I said gruffly.

"Hi," he replied. Such a one-word maestro.

"Cell phone works, huh? Thought it might be broke."

I didn't need to wait for the next single-syllable response. Tammy called from the kitchen,

"Blake, can you come here?"

I unbuckled my holster and swung it over my shoulder.

Tammy prefers her husband unarmed when we have our discussions, silly to me but understandable. I held it out to her as I came into the kitchen.

"Here you go, Madam Armorer."

She didn't take it. She didn't even look at me.

"We have to talk. I—"

"Listen," I cut in, "I've had a real bad day and tomorrow's going to be worse. So, whatever you…"

She made a beeline for the back door and burst outside. I took a deep breath and almost went for the sleeping bag but instead stepped out after her.

"Hey," I said when I got into the yard, "you probably heard Mariel's kid's dead. Been on it all day, and I'm way past exhausted. You should've just stayed at your—"

"Come here."

Tammy retrieved a pack of cigarettes from her car. She started smoking again last year, and since she was going to puff away, I figured it was a good time to jump off the wagon myself.

I gave a half-smile and reached out my hand. "Lemme have one."

"Look."

She pointed down. The night was dark except for a little moonlight, but I hardly needed any to match the real thing perfectly to the image in my mind. Solid impact damage to the passenger front end, almost within an inch of where I'd imagined it.

"Cliff swears he wasn't drunk. He said it was dark and slippery and after…he was just scared. He didn't…"

Her words flew past me. I was trying to speak but my head was pounding and all I could think about was that mirror in the bar earlier today and how it looked so different on the other side.

"Blake, you have to do something."

Tammy was talking to the wrong man. The man she wanted was on the other side of the glass. When she stepped up and put her trembling hands to my face, I knew she had already chosen which suffering was worse.

"Do something," she pleaded.

I did. I hugged her long and tight. She then went in to check on Cliff and I smoked a cigarette right down to the filter.

Except for a few mostly imagined scares in my young life, fear has never been a sensation that has touched me, let alone take hold with its icy fingers. But now, my mouth had gone dry as cotton, and beads of sweat broke out on my forehead. Even the crisp night air was difficult to breathe. I told myself that this was as bad as it could get, and the next best move is to not even speak about the horror so fresh in my mind, ticking away like a nuclear detonator. Instead, I went into the house. After telling Tammy and Cliff, without looking them in the eye, that I was going to take care of things, I grabbed a sleeping bag from the closet and headed out to the truck.

Chapter Two

Even though bone-tired, I spent twenty minutes heating up the truck and at least an hour rolling around trying to get comfortable on the crew cab seats. Whenever I'd drift into a doze, the events at hand would snap me awake, but eventually I fell under.

It seemed no time had passed when I awoke with a start, gasping for breath as if the planet's atmosphere had just collapsed and I had precious few seconds left to live. During the tortured nap, I'd been dreaming about Tammy and Cliff. We were at the beach on a hot summer day, Tammy sitting on a blanket and laughing as I chased Cliff around with a long piece of seaweed. Suddenly, we were at some kind of castle, and there was this big dining room full of food, and the three of us stuffed our faces until, out of nowhere, Cliff began stabbing me with a long knife. I did nothing while he kept hacking away, and I guess it hurt because I screamed myself awake.

When I sat up, I could hardly remember the dream at all, although it came to me in more detail after I climbed out of the sleeping bag and began rubbing away the condensation on the window for a long stare up into the starry night sky. The most vivid part was my son's eyes. Although blurred by a dreamy fuzz that made everything feel odd, there was no look of violence in them at all, just terribly sad and lost and scared.

A loud tapping at the front window startled the hell out of me.

"Blake. Blake!" Tammy hissed in the night like the feline she surely is. She's about the only person in the world who can sneak up on me. "Wake up!"

I knocked on the back window and bunched up the sleeping bag as if trying to snooze during a crisis were a shameful act. "I'm back here."

She pulled the driver's door open but didn't get in. The cold air rushed through the cabin and jarred me fully awake, into the crappiest of all moods. Tammy looked like she'd also spent the last two plus hours anxiously coaxing sleep in vain.

"Come in the house," she demanded in a bothered whisper.

"No fucking way," I whispered back. There's no neighbor within acres, but I strangely played along. "I'm staying here."

Tammy let out a huge huff and jumped inside, slamming the door shut. After she climbed in the back, I slid as far away from her on the bench seat as I could but tossed the sleeping bag over. Never one to leave her own comfort unattended, she quickly spread it out yet left a wide corner of it for me to cover my legs. Old matrimonial habits die hard.

"So? What are you going to do?"

"I don't know," I barked at her. "That's why I need time to think."

"To think?" She put on a familiar shocked face. It comes mainly when she's at a loss for what to say, a deer in the headlights of self-expression. "I told you what happened. Wait. You are *not* talking about arresting him."

"The legal responsibility is—"

"Fuck the law, Blake!" she reached out and grabbed my arm, and I let her. "You…*we* need to help him. We need to fix this. We have to—"

"Teach him right from wrong."

A heavy silence fell, the kind in which so much is communicated. Tammy stared at me, and I heard her thoughts as if they were screaming inside my own head, yet I let her stew in her pot of warming manipulation. Hell, she deserved a good cooking after taking off with Cliff after something like this. It only made a shitty situation much, much worse.

"You want me to get him off somehow," I whispered, "but it doesn't work like that."

"This isn't work! It's your family!"

"He killed a kid, Tammy."

"It was an accident!" She wanted to scream but checked it in a frantic squeal. "Why ruin two lives? You could…"

Ripping the sleeping bag off my legs, I slid away from her, bumping hard into the side panel. The truck was now just as cold as outside, and the imitation leather crackled under my weight. The mist appeared and vanished inches in front of Tammy's mouth, but her words had nothing but fire in them.

"Go ahead. Run away. Like you have from everything."

"The hell you talking about? You're the one who takes off to your mother's every month so you can fuck around."

"You never cared about being a husband or a father. Your whole life is right here, in your truck. Running off and helping other people instead of being a man and protecting your home."

"You're the one who runs away. Maybe the kid would have a backbone if his mother didn't teach him that cheating and lying is part of being family."

"Fuck you!" She struck a backhand against my arm. "You can save us! And you don't want to! You don't care! Selfish! Selfish!!"

She balled her hands into little fists and let loose with a barrage of blows to my shoulder. Only when she landed a punch to the side of my head did I grab both of her arms and shout straight into her face.

"You wrecked our life, not me! He's a good kid who got taught how to be bad!"

I let go of her arms, and she curled up into a ball, hugging the sleeping bag tight to her body while she released stifled sobs into its fabric. I wanted to reach out and comfort her, but all the other things that I really want to do, like fix this whole mess and make it go away, were piling up right behind that one gesture, so instead I sat straight in the seat and bit my lip until she got a hold of herself.

"Don't you have any tissues in this rig?" she asked, sitting up and wiping her face with a jacket arm, then looking around incredulously.

I grabbed some old bakery napkins out of the console storage box. I wouldn't touch her again, but I could try to calm her.

"Those are left over from two honey-dipped crullers," I advised, "so don't be shocked if you get some dried-up glaze on you. It's good for the pores, though."

She didn't laugh. She also didn't hit me again. I had such an urge to take her into the house and get underneath a pile of blankets on the couch and let this night pass with no decisions at all. We were already at the end of our marriage and Cliff going off to school was somehow the unmentioned finish line but we were a couple of struggling runners who hadn't trained enough before the race, limping along in pain and regret, attempting with feeble honor to close out a competition beyond our physical and mental powers.

She finally broke the silence. "What if we went away? Canada or…"

"I can't go anywhere."

"Not you," She let her words fall with full knowledge of their damage. "I'd take him somewhere and start over. I don't mean my mom's. Far away."

"You'll be a suspect. So will Cliff. You can't run from these things."

"I could try. Until he's old enough to..."

I hit the back of the headrest hard with a closed fist. Tammy jumped in her seat and it felt so good that I hammered on it several more times.

"What kind of man are you talking about raising?! Running away after killing a kid and carrying around a mess of guilt his whole life? Who's he gonna be? Huh? What kind of future starts that way? What the fuck, Tammy!"

She turned to face the window, and I did the same on the opposite side. Suddenly, everything I ever did wrong as a father raced through my mind, not enough discipline, too much discipline, long stretches of absences, too intense punishment for misbehavior. It all seemed like one colossal failure on my part. Maybe that's why I was so torn, spinning wheels in a deep muck of judgment—of myself as well as my son.

"It's my fault," Tammy whispered.

"Now don't climb up on a cross. We've got to…"

"It's all my fault," she said with more conviction.

"Listen, I'm going through the same thing in my head, and it won't do us any good. We've got to solve this problem as best we can for Cliff."

"Then why can't we make it go away!"

"Because there's a family out there who lost their kid. Put yourself in their place. Someone runs down Cliff. What would you do? Huh?"

"That's your fucking job talking," she muttered. "You can't ever get away from it. Not even to save your son from hell. You are so far away from the man I married that—"

The squelch of the two-way radio startled Tammy way more than it did me. It has basically wormed its way into my brain like a personal ringtone.

"Sheriff, you out there, over?" Stacey's voice was tired and yet more alive than anyone in this truck. "Sheriff, we got a situation."

I leaned up and grabbed the receiver while Tammy reached over and opened the driver's door.

"Nothing more important than work."

"Just wait a second, will you?" I turned and put a light hand on her knee, "This could be about all this shit."

Tammy tugged the door closed but sat back and upright with such tension I imagined her next exit would involve exploding through the roof of the truck.

"Stacey, it's Blake, what's up, over?" I pressed the handset to my cheek and lowered my head, waiting for worse news to come my way.

"Hey, Sheriff, you weren't texting back. Have you been out night-drivin' again, over?" Stacey had a bad habit of chit-chatting, especially on the two-way.

"Stace, I shut my phone off, just tell me the deal!" I held the handset so close to my teeth that I could bite through it.

"Sorry! I…yeh, there's a home invasion out at Franklin Pond."

"What?"

Due to its proneness to flood during wet winters, there are only two dwellings out at Franklin Pond. One's a small shack owned by Red Kelsy that he uses to store fishing gear and bottles of scotch. The other's an old lady in a country house, built wisely a hundred years ago on a hill with a solid rock plateau, keeping the place safe and dry during tempests that have carried away her neighbors' homes. She's a simple old lady, and as far as I know the only threat to invade her house is carpenter ants and wasps.

"It's a bear, Sheriff…over."

"Oh, great," I exhaled.

Despite my exhaustion, I figured answering a call might be the best thing for my spinning head right now. The dead of night has always had a recuperating effect on me, likely fostered after my parents had exhausted the life out of each other in drawn-out screaming matches that erupted into brief yet brutal physical altercations. When the tumult woke me, I'd crawl out of my second-floor window and up onto the scratchy shingled-roof, where on warmer nights I'd lie and stare at the black night or cloud-covered sky. My parents never knew I was out there but I forgave their cluelessness. I don't think they really knew each other so much, either. Stealing a glance at Tammy, sitting cross armed, steaming mad yet silent, I wondered if all marriages are just cut from different pieces of the same old, tattered cloth.

"Mrs. Jenkins called from her car. Said the bear is in the kitchen, over."

"I'm on it. Ten to twelve minutes transit."

"The bears are early this year, most times—"

"Educate me later, Stacey," I said with tender bluntness before she could launch into a blather about Ursidae hibernation patterns. "Over and out."

I tossed the handset onto the front seat and turned to Tammy.

"I gotta go."

"To arrest a bear?" she replied and stared straight through me. "You'd rather fight a bear than save your family."

"She's an old lady. It's cold."

I threw my door open, stepped out and got a taste of the raw night. Spring never seems to start until it's almost summer around here. Tammy got out on her side and came around the back wrapped in the sleeping bag.

"We'll talk after," I assured her.

"We might talk but you won't budge. I swear, Blake, this is like the grand finale of all the ways you've let us down over the years. You try to arrest my son and I swear I'll take him away forever. Forever!"

She spun around and headed into the house. Fortunately, I didn't need to follow. I had my holster and gun with me. More importantly, I knew that if I did go in there, the battle that followed would go on for a long time. It's just the way my wife and I have always done things from Day One.

Tammy moved to town in my senior year of high school and we managed to have a fling or two before I graduated. She was the kind of petite, dark-haired cute that could turn down-right sexy at the drop of a hat but also with enough smarts to talk about all kinds of things. Still, small-town fate kept us apart until years later when I started hanging around *Deuces Wild* and a few steamy after-hours flings turned into something pretty heavy, so heavy that we eventually sunk into marriage and continued downward into uncharted depths of acrimony. But the treasure we managed to pull up from the marital sea bottom is our boy, Cliff. Always the cutest little kid and now a handsome young man set to attend college in New Hampshire in the fall, that is until this whole terrible mess exploded in our faces.

As I tore down the driveway, it occurred to me with bitterness that Tammy was exactly right. If the choice is to either toss and turn inside a cold truck until sunrise when I'm legally bound to wake up my son and arrest him for manslaughter or go off into the dead of night fight a hungry bear, I'll take the bear every fucking time.

* * *

I never minded getting roused from bed by a distress call in the wee hours when I first signed up as a sheriff's deputy. Back then, no matter the nocturnal mischief conducted by man or beast, I'd happily strap on the gun and go break up whatever young people's after-hours party got too raucous or blow an air horn into an attic to disperse overactive raccoons. It was great part-time employment between commuting to Farmingdale for college and driving out to the academy at Vassalboro for the required training. Still, the work stayed firmly tucked away into the 'temporary' file of my life plans until Sheriff Bueker passed away a little over a year into my job. Suddenly, I was sworn in as sheriff and, although I figured the next election would cure me of that, the town overwhelmingly voted for me repeatedly. My mom was still alive in those days and in pretty much financial ruin, so I needed the money. Also, some of the candidates that ran against me were either thieves from birth or life-long psychopaths, which added a strong dose of civic guilt to my decision to say goodbye to college and hello cramped existence in the small and stagnant world of Rock Hollow, Maine, a tiny town stuck in the mid-20th century until the state put up a giant cell tower about thirty miles west to keep motorists on the interstate from getting lost because GPS kicked out. Now Rock Hollow is still a backwoods village but a little less sleepy under a constant online blanket of videos, emails, and data streams.

Spurred by the town's great technological advancements in communication, midnight distress calls about bears are plentiful until they go into hibernation. After that, folks get busy with crises of their own making like running portable generators in their kitchen during a power outage. Truth told, the bears aren't the problem. They've been doing their thing for hundreds of thousands of years with no discernible destruction of the planet or each other. People are a far different story. You can't walk down Main St. on an April morning without overhearing someone complaining about the damn bears invading their property. Most times it's because they left garbage lying around outside or had a barbeque grill that hadn't been cleaned since purchase. Then there's the numbskull who thinks it's fun to leave buckets of kibble on their lawn and snap pictures of the cute, three-hundred-pound ball of fuzz, claws and teeth that soon appears to gobble it up.

Rarely discussed is the high intelligence within those big furry heads. If you ever underestimated a three-year-old who will climb to get to the cookie jar on top of the refrigerator, then you will be flabbergasted at the six different ways to Sunday that a bear will invent to get into a house that has baked goods, animal food, or even just old, rotting garbage in a back room waiting for dump-run day. Based on the average brainpower of some people around town, we might be better off letting the bears have the homes and setting the clueless folks out into the wild.

When I reached the Jenkins property, I pulled in with siren blaring and lights flashing in hope that it might scare the bear out of the house without me having to leave the truck. I eased up alongside Mrs. Jenkin's white SUV and found her in the front seat holding a large pot and a frying pan, which she discarded to roll her window down. The poor old lady was only in her nightgown, looking so scared that I cut the siren but kept the flashers on.

"Oh, Sheriff, thank heavens!" She couldn't get the words out fast enough. "I heard such a racket in the kitchen, and I just knew it was a bear. I never leave the windows open, but the air's so stuffy inside from burning wood all day, so I figured what's the harm? Well, that son-of-a-bitch is in there wrecking the place! And I don't know where my cats are!"

Mrs. Jenkins was always crazy but only in a passive way such as wearing a man's tuxedo to the Fourth of July fireworks or spray painting 'onion' in fat letters on the side of her vehicle. No one's figured that one out yet. Most of her antics began after she lost her husband to cancer a couple of years back. Because I once had a bat-shit crazy grandma myself, I had a soft spot for local aging nuts.

"Don't worry, ma'am." I tried to ease her nerves with an officer-in-charge voice, undermined by the nervous way I scanned the windows of the two rooms that had lights on. "You're sure it's a bear?"

"Of course it's a bear!" she shouted, shaking the frying pan. "I don't bang pans for raccoons!"

"OK, OK, take it easy. I'll have a look." I suddenly remembered how difficult some older folks can be in a crisis, almost as if they're embarrassed to ask for help.

I got out of the truck, keeping an eye on the front door and windows as I made my way to the rear of the vehicle. "Is there a back door?"

"Yes, but it's been stuck shut forever. My husband was supposed to fix it, but then he died. Sheriff, I got to look for my cats!"

"Mrs. Jenkins, one problem at a time, please." Another way out of the house would've been helpful for both me and the animal. The danger of this set-up was becoming real and I tried to keep my concern behind a warm smile. "It won't bother your cats. Bears are sort of like big cats themselves. Anyway, I need you to stay in the car with the windows up and let me take care of things."

"What if it kills you?"

I looked her kindly in the eyes. She meant nothing by it. Same as my old grandma telling me that grandpa liked to have sex in the tub. Just wild words that mean nothing in the end, except ensuring that I took only showers for the rest of my life.

"Then maybe you can be the next sheriff." Her face lit up for a second or two, savoring the thought before my semi-stern demand. "So, roll those windows up, please."

She did as instructed while I popped open the back of the truck to grab a can of bear-spray, a shotgun, and extra shells. I almost went for the rifle, as putting a shot in the animal could scare it off but a trapped bear will eat a rifle for lunch. My Remington pump-action, loaded with heavy-hitter slugs, makes far better odds to save my skin, if it comes to that. The truth is that I don't want it to. I've never shot any animal other than deer in my life and even those gave me strong pangs of guilt when they take too long to die.

Finally, I strapped on a headlamp and cranked the beam up high, beginning a careful approach to towards the house.

When I glanced back at Mrs. Jenkins, her face was pressed up to the window, twisted in concern and bathed in my headlamp's eerie light. She sort of resembled a circus freak.

"It's OK. If you see him run out, then beep your horn. Understand?"

She gave the car horn a blast, and I returned a thumbs up. Nearing the house, I thought I saw a shadow moving inside but couldn't be sure. I began shouting and banging the butt of the shotgun against a porch beam. Since no one was coming out, I started to climb the steps while belting out an old song to spook the animal.

"*Well, you wake up in the mornin',*" I sang tunelessly, putting a heavy boot down on each step up, "*you hear the work bell ring...*"

Up on the porch, I had a much better look through the front door that Mrs. Jenkins had left open in her haste. Like many of the older places on the mountain, built with lumber felled, milled, and finished locally, the dwelling was a simple two-story farmhouse. Four or five rooms below and the same up top, discounting any kind of dug basement.

With my back against the porch wall, I slowly peered inside and let the headlamp illuminate the hallway and a staircase leading up to the second floor that I prayed our furry friend hadn't used.

"Do me a favor, big old bear," I thought, "and forget about which bed is too soft, too hard or just right. How about getting back to outside business, like chasing Goldilocks' ass through the woods?"

Casting the beam straight down the hallway into the kitchen, the light revealed two cabinet doors recently ripped off their hinges and what looked to be a mess of boxes and bags torn apart on the floor. A brief cacophony of cracking wood and scraping came from somewhere deep inside the house until the uncanny white noise of silence took over again.

I stomped on the porch a bunch more times, then took a big, deep breath before stepping across the threshold with the shotgun readied, crooked in one arm. With each slow step forward, my free hand was itching to deploy the spray if I was afforded the luxury of a good twenty feet between me and the bear. Imagining such a showdown made me wish that I ditched my heavy coat to allow quicker motions.

"And they march you to the table…you see the same old thing."

Just as I reached the end of the hall, a good deal more clatter began coming from the other side of the house. An active feller for sure. Of course, with my ongoing luck, I'd draw a Type A bear. With my back pressed against the wall, I peered around the corner and flicked a switch on a nearby pane, illuminating the kitchen with a tiny lamp near the stove, enough dim light to confirm the room to be absent of woodland creatures and one holy hell of a mess. Any food items that hadn't been stored in the cabinets were torn from their package, bag or box and strewn about while everything from the floor to the table, counters and sink were covered in what must have once been a gigantic bag of flour.

"Ain't no food upon the table. And no pork up in the pan," I croaked.

On the linoleum floor, near my foot stood a busted ceramic bowl licked almost clean of batter, so I picked it up and fired it across the kitchen at the entryway to the next room to scare up some action but no sign of the suspect who had entered the premises through a window to the right of that doorway, leaving the screen mangled on the floor along with broken pieces of sash and glass, and the entire wood frame cracked and hanging. It's best to keep clear of the entrance that the animal has used because they have smarts enough to get back out the same way. In this case, there was no getting to the rest of the house without passing the broken window, adding a high probability of my cornering the bear, just the kind of thing I love to do in the middle of the night with a rising case of nerves.

"*But you better not complain, boy. You get in trouble with the man.*" A dry mouth and throat greatly impaired my a cappella performance.

A rapid thudding came from the back of the house, where the bear was panting heavily, probably trying to get through the door the dead husband had never fixed. Keeping as clear of the busted window as possible, I crept over to the passage and craned my neck to get some light into the next room, which was more of a rectangular shape than the kitchen. Still no animal in sight.

The commotion deeper in the house carried on for several more seconds, and I really didn't care if it knocked the entire wall down as long as it got out. Then the sound of more wood crunching and loud growls and huffs alarmed me enough to reach for the spray, but as soon as my fingers wrapped around the cold steel of the canister, the house went quiet for a few long seconds until the old lady's car horn signified that the bear had made it outside. Finally, a fucking blast of good luck!

I took a few deep breaths of air to relieve the tension in my chest. Now it was apparent I would survive this detail, my mind raced right back to Cliff. I had this job to finish, and it would at least give me a little time to rationalize my fucked-up family situation, so before going out to secure the yard, I quickly surveyed the damage the animal left behind inside. Moving with caution, I stepped into the next room which was sort of a parlor, stuffed with chairs, tables, and footstools. Adjoining it was an awkwardly built addition and the location of the famous unusable back door, now boasting a fresh opening the size of a manhole cover at its base. I tracked my light across the chunks of wood and a small torn leather flap on the floor, the remnants of what must have been a pet door for the old lady's cats. Since Mrs. Jenkins was still leaning on the horn outside, this call's next and far easier phase will be calming her down with the good news and getting the house secure.

Before I could step into the kitchen, the sound of cracking wood came from the mudroom, with a sort of popping noise. I spun around to see the bear coming straight at me. Its hairy black mass filled up the room but for the flicker of the headlamp bouncing off the whites of its eyes. The snout opened in a horrible growl of big, curled pink tongue and sharp yellowed teeth. I took an instant step back, but before I could point the gun at the bear, my boot came down on a footstool and l stumbled, spilling to the floor.

Amid absolute panic, everything around me swam in a thick, ancient aroma of earth and pungent sweat. The bear's belly grazed my chest and face as it leaped over me and landed in the kitchen. I stayed stock-still lying on my back without daring even a breath while the beast forcefully grunted and let out another long, ferocious growl. My hand lay several inches from the spray cannister on my belt, but my brain somehow worked just a hair faster and stopped me from grabbing it.

Then, just like that, I was alone, lying motionless, not even breathing until I had to roll over and suck in a few large, gulping gasps of air. The old lady continued blasting the car horn outside, and my heart was beating like a war drum. The trembling began in my hands, climbed up my arms, and ran all the way down my back.

Finally, I grabbed the shotgun and got up, remembering my responsibilities, concerned suddenly that the bear might go after Mrs. Jenkins. Who knew what kind of snacks she's got stored in that car? I flew through the kitchen and down the hallway, jumping out onto the porch and nearly losing my balance.

The bear had not run off yet. And it wasn't alone.

Big Mama was pacing back and forth on a flattened patch of dead leaves beside a small tool shed, plenty far away from Mrs. Jenkins' car. Two little bear cubs were nearby, one pawing at the shed and the other near the fringe of the woods, about ten feet off the ground, holding tight to the trunk of a fir tree. I kept the headlamp shining on her as she grunted at the first cub and then made her way over to the one up the tree, turning to glance between me and Mrs. Jenkins several times. Now standing on her hind legs at the base of the trunk, the bear whimpered and pulled at the little one to come down, a simple action that took my breath away. This mama bear had stuck inside the house until her babies were safely out, even as a clumsy human approached armed with mace and bullets, and now she wasn't going anywhere without both of her cubs. We occupy a small part in these creatures' constant idyll of feeding and nuzzling and gentle slumber. I could picture them all in some narrow cave up the mountain, little furry babes pressing up against their warm mom, entirely unaware of lethal worldly distractions like greed, jealousy, and sin. Damn it, now I was sort of choked up. What the fuck is wrong with me?

Shaking myself out of this sudden rush of emotion, I extended one arm with a flat-palmed wave toward the old lady, and she kept tight inside the car while thankfully ceasing to blare on the horn. With the other arm, I brought the gun up slowly, my fingers were numb with cold and stung sharply when I got off the first shot. Scared by the gunfire, the little bear still didn't come down from the tree, and Mama gave me a real dark look, so I fired another two warning shots into the air. Finally, after she clawed her way up and yanked the cub to the ground, the three of them went scampering off together into the woods.

Watching them go, I thought about how Mama Bear will have to part with her two little ones in another year, when they'll go their way and she'll go hers, but for now she is loving the shit out of her babies like there's no tomorrow. Not too many animals, or people for that matter, ever allow themselves that type of pure love. I pulled myself together as best I could before walking over to let Mrs. Jenkins out of her car.

"My God there was an army of em'!" she shouted as I led her over to the house.

"You shoulda shot the whole bunch!"

"It was just a mother and her cubs." I looked back at the wood line where they had disappeared, really hoping to catch one last glimpse of them.

"Shoot em all!" she screamed into the air, pausing on the top step as a set of trembles overtook her shoulders.

Once I got Mrs. Jenkins calmed down on the front porch, and then all over again in the kitchen after she'd seen the mess the animals had made, she showed me where her hammer and nails were stored and directed me to a pile of lumber pieces in the shed outside. She promised to stay inside her bedroom while I patched up the window and hole in the door until a contractor could get there tomorrow to do it right.

Before setting into some hasty carpentry, I went out to the truck and got my cell phone and moved over near the pine tree where the bears had been. After thinking really hard for a few moments, I took a deep breath of chilly night air and dialed Tammy.

She answered within a couple of rings but mumbled sleepily, "Mmmhh. What'shh it?"

"Get rid of the car," I said before kneeling at the base of the tree, touching some claw marks left in the bark where the mama and cub had been climbing. "Do it right now. Drive to your mother's or…I don't care. Don't tell me anything. Just get rid of it."

She sounded much more awake now. "Wait. What am I supposed—"

"Do it," I said gruffly and hung up before she could get either one of us thinking too much.

Then I stood and went to patch up the house, wondering the whole time about how much worse things could've gone here tonight and how bad things will still get, knowing events are about to turn fucking sinister. I fell into hammering some nails while ignoring the old lady's shrieking demands from upstairs to go outside and look for her cats, instead focusing hard on the tune playing a nervous loop inside of my head, thankfully keeping the other grim, dark thoughts at bay until some kind of plan started coming together. Because there had to be one. There had to be.

"Let the midnight special shine a light on me. Let the midnight special shine a ever lovin' light on me…"

Chapter Three

It took way longer than expected to secure Mrs. Jenkin's house, mainly due to tracking down her damn cats in the woods for almost an hour. By the time the three of them were safe and sound in the kitchen lapping up an early breakfast, the sun was just making its way above the horizon. The property commanded a great morning view, with the mountains in the distance and the pond below catching the early daylight, beginning the transformation from night's black to a slate gray with thin strips of ice on its banks, the passing season holding on with a cold, brittle grip.

After packing my gear into the truck, I considered going home to check on the progress of the dirty deed assigned to Tammy but daytime was here, and with it a kettle of trouble brewing in town, which would likely blow its top once the Hinckle brothers arrived. Even this blissful morning moment in nature felt as if it could explode in my face, so I got in the truck. If the brothers were still in transit, then my first stop would be the diner for a couple of cups of seriously strong coffee and maybe some breakfast to keep mind and body geared up.

Driving down the turnpike back into town, the truly gorgeous dawn casting its orange fire across the land seemed to mock the severity of my mood. The quiet woods with light green buds appearing on tree branches, and still bodies of water reflecting a near perfect image of the mountains and sky, only increased the knot in my stomach and tightness in my chest, like I was becoming some sort of Frankenstein's monster who got himself a little knowledge and understood that the world is full of nothing but pain and suffering.

A hot flash of annoyance shot through me at the sight of two familiar vehicles sitting outside the diner. Parked right behind a gas guzzling oversized SUV belonging to Melvin Pyles, the town supervisor, sat an absurd-looking electric truck, the modern must-have vehicle for the well-to-do and perpetually reaching crowd, resembling an illicit offspring of a lunar buggy and an abhorrent parade float, thrown together using scrap metal from a junkyard. The only person driving one in these parts is yet another town council member and Melvin's puppet master, Lydia Bernard, who Tammy dubbed "The Wicked Witch of the Worst."

Melvin and Lydia are without question the bane of my professional existence in Rock Hollow. Their seemingly life-long positions as two of the Town Board's three members have kept a vice grip over local politics since the third member, Charlie Langer, resigned in utter disgust at the pair and moved to Florida, replaced by John Camponelli, a friend of mine and the local oil delivery tycoon, who only cares about covering up industrial spills and couldn't give a fig about municipal bullshit. Through small-town budgetary chicanery, the Board had rejected by two to one any increase in my salary and benefits for the past three years, even though both are paltry compared to the compensation packages other sheriffs earn throughout the state. Whenever I brought up a sorely needed increase in pay, their tactic was to besiege me with all the town's issues, such as boisterous teens and young adults partying at the quarry on the weekends and the increase of vaping at the high school. However, their biggest gripe was the lack of traffic control when the Board stages their heavily marketed and poorly planned seasonal events, such as a Midsummer Picnic or an Autumn Oktoberfest or tomorrow's Spring Maple Syrup festival, each a celebration that the wealthy denizens throw to bring together the common folks of Rock Hollow, so the countrified hoi polloi can sit in cordoned off VIP sections and hob-knob at safe distances from the peasants.

Despite the manufactured snobbery, the events always attract large crowds because nothing else goes on around here besides a high school basketball game in the winter and the beer-soaked adult town softball league in the summer. The heavy festival attendance is despite the fact that after tickets to get in, exorbitantly priced plates of food, and tents designed to force you and the last cash in your wallet to part ways so your kids can buy some artisan trinkets, also known as rocks, that supposedly bring good luck, the average family comes out of one these "community events" having been fleeced of a week's grocery bill. At the last one, a magician performed in the VIP area. If they couldn't afford the extra twenty bucks a head, the kids from the poorer families had to stand and watch outside the makeshift orange mesh carnival fence, excluded like a bunch of little lepers. I remember wanting to grab that motherfucker Mr. Presto's magic wand and use it to make our two fatheaded, myopic figures of town leadership disappear into thin air.

Melvin Pyles runs a highly profitable tree removal business which he inherited from his father, a man formerly known as the nicest man in town. Melvin did not, however, inherit his father's temperament. When a real bad storm blows through and huge trunks and limbs are down everywhere, his company comes to the rescue of only the homes that can pay their bills, which are jacked up to exorbitant rates due to a local monopoly arranged by the Board's hastily approved and highly suspect town ordinances regarding tree-removal licenses. So, if you live in a low income house like well over half the folks around here and a tropical storm makes a surprising push north, landing an oak in your living room, you better hope for a declaration of disaster so the state of Maine can pay Melvin Pyles to help his neighbor. Most times, me and a half-dozen guys called the "Chainsaw Gang" end up heading out and clearing the dangerous messes pro bono. A mean middle-aged man, Pyles is on his way to becoming an elderly son-of-a-bitch who barely hides his hostility behind the hallmark greetings of a dirty politician—a grit-toothed grin and vigorous handshakes held way too long. It's a shame, because his wife is kind of OK, in a bible-thumping sort of way, and their two girls are quiet but well-behaved grade schoolers. I suppose we give those kids a few teenage years to get a good picture of their old man before they rebel against his shit-ass ways and, with any luck, topple from within the closest thing that Rock Hollow has to a tyrant.

As for the other constant pain in my ass, what can be said about Lydia Bernard that I've not already said a hundred times? Nothing good, that's for damn sure. To give a decent picture of her personality and physical resemblance look to the freak creatures of nature, and particularly the genus Rana Palustris, more commonly known as a dart frog. With a highly toxic and casually abusive approach to life, Lydia takes great pains to be in everybody's business, along with a small cabal of friends, similarly ugly, in appearance and demeanor. They secrete jealous gossip in whispers and hateful libel in screeches toward any rival opposition in their path, quite often simply the town's other, prettier wives. Victims of not maturing past the age of high school mean girls, these grown ladies all married wealthy, unattractive husbands and, unlike the Pyles household, most of their kids are trouble-makers and spoiled brats, all following patterns in delusional self-importance laid down like slime trails by the giant poisonous frog, Lydia.

Following an unscrupulous path into small-town politics, which often works well across this great country of ours, Lydia forced her way into a position of local leadership. She did so not by taking over a family business, like Pyles but via her, father's fortune, made in the great state of New York, where the old man is still incarcerated for orchestrating a massive Ponzi scheme that removed the shirts from hundreds of thousands of elderly investors. Prior to moving to Rock Hollow, Lydia somehow neutralized her toxins for the duration of the courtship and married Willem Bernard, the only son of a Vermont dairy industry executive, rumored to have made a small fortune by getting into yogurt early. As father and son were barely on speaking terms, the old man cut the new couple a very big check in exchange for leaving him alone. So, the newlyweds cooked up the idea that, instead of being so-so wealthy in the city, they would instead move north to New England and pose as country squires. To my misfortune, they chose Rock Hollow, to establish the front of wilderness aristocracy, buying up the grounds of the old burned-down hotel on Tanner Mountain. There they set about knocking down about a thousand trees, all over three hundred years old, and built an enormous reception hall with some adjoining cabins. Then they dug an in-ground pool, cleared space for tennis courts, stuck some croquet hoops in the grass, and opened the district's first ever country club. Of course, only the area's upper-class families, a smallish mix of old money, new money, and illegal money, pay the outrageous annual fee that allows them to swim in the pool in the summer, when both the temperature and humidity are well over ninety, while the rest of us cool off our overheated carcasses in one of a half-dozen big creeks outside of town. It's another example of the have and have-nots, but the simple truth is that you can't be a have-not if you just don't give a fuck what the haves have, which is why those of us who hang at the creeks refer to the Pure Gold Acres Country Club as "For Old Fakers."

Instead of risking a loss of appetite in the presence of Melvin and Lydia, the alternative was to turn around, drive home, and see if Tammy had actually taken care of business and lost the car. But considering the early hour, I preferred to gamble on being able to digest the presence of town board members alongside a big dish of scrambled eggs and hash.

When I stepped into the diner, I couldn't even give a proper "hey" to Sam before Pyles and Lydia tried to catch my attention by motioning me over to their corner table. My pretending not to see them forced Lydia to fill the air with a harsh demand.

"Sheriff, come here, please? We have a problem."

Besides those two at the table and Sam behind the counter, there was only one other person in the place. Henry Struthers orders two doughnuts and coffee every day like clockwork at 05:15 before going next door to open the hardware store. Henry was just preparing to leave and gave me a "you poor SOB" look, which I returned with a wave. Henry hates Lydia with passion, going years back to when she stiffed payment to a large group of contractors working on her new club, who in turn refused to pay Henry for the tools and materials they'd purchased on credit, backed of course by the poison frog. When Henry drove a trailer to the club to reclaim his stock, Lydia called me to arrest him for trespassing. So, I hustled up there and put Henry in cuffs and then drove him home, where we drank a few beers. He finally hired a city lawyer and sued Lydia to get his stuff back.

"Hell is too good a place for that woman," Henry remarked as he passed me on the way out.

I finally greeted the proprietor, "Hey, Sam, can I get a massive cup of coffee?"

"Comin' right up." He winked and added a whispered jibe of, "I'll bring it over to your little party."

"Thanks, bud." I gave him a feigned look of frustration before I walked over to the inquisitor's table, and the real thing spread across my face. "You folks are up early."

The two of them looked like a bizarre version of Abbott and Costello, he of the thin frame and even thinner gray hair; she resembling a blonde-haired, pinched-faced baker who had gotten way too high on their own supply of cupcakes.

"Sit down, Blake," Pyles muttered out of the corner of his mouth, "this isn't a social occasion."

"That's good," I replied while pulling out a chair for myself, "I'm not feeling particularly social."

I sat down, and Sam brought me a steaming mug of coffee, kindly pouring it into the big ceramic cups he uses for soup. Pyles and Lydia held their coordinated assault until Sam had returned behind the counter.

"What the hell is going on with the hit and run?" Pyles sputtered, hanging his neck down toward his coffee cup, yet looking up with wide, accusative eyes.

"This is a disaster, Sheriff," Lydia hissed, pushing away a plate that held only an abandoned muffin wrapper. "The Maple Syrup Festival starts at noon, and you've got the whole town in an uproar because—"

"Doesn't exactly look like pandemonium," I interrupted, glancing around the empty diner.

"Oh, please," Lydia growled with such vigor that I was surprised she was only drinking tea. "The state police are on their way, I heard. And the Hinckle brothers? We praised the day that those goons left town, and now they're coming back like a group of…uh, you know…"

"Vigilantes," Pyles said, saving Lydia from her limited vocabulary.

"Exactly. Vigilantes. Why can't you do your job and keep the peace around here?"

I took a big sip of hot coffee and stared silently at the two of them.

"Well?" Pyles demanded. "Are you going to find out who killed that boy?"

"Been up all night thinking about it," I replied, the black irony of my words sending a shudder down my spine.

"Well, stop thinking and do something." Lydia grabbed the spoon out of her tea and dropped it on the table. "We *pay* you to keep people happy, and people are not happy right now!"

"I'm not a circus clown, Lydia," I replied coolly, although I honestly felt like screaming out the guilt in my gut. "Folks want happiness, they need to start in their own homes."

"The hell is that supposed to mean? Listen, I'm a businesswoman and…"

She drew a deep breath in preparation to unleash a torrent of hot air. Lydia's famous words before she climbs up on the cross are always, "I'm a businesswoman," even though she lives fifteen miles away from her business and only appears once a week to drop off paychecks or threaten to fire employees without cause.

"...I know people. I deal with them every day. And this afternoon if state police are sniffing around town and mentally deranged brothers are pulling off crazy-ass antics, people won't want maple syrup! Do you know how much I've done to make this festival happen?"

"How much," I snapped back at her in full knowledge that she ran the festival like her country club, cutting checks and hiring temporary staff to pull off the event. "Do you know Alice Donovan?"

"Who?"

"Alice Donovan. She's the manager at the Mill Restaurant? They'll be cooking up all those pancakes you'll be stuffing yourself with."

"If I hired her, then I know her. Besides—"

"No, you don't. But she sure knows you."

"She knows …listen I'm not taking any more of your—"

Pyles put a hand up between the flush-cheeked Lydia and me. "Whoa, now. Let's not turn this into a shitshow. Blake, you need to wrap this thing up. Today."

"That's easy to say, but—"

"No damned buts," Pyles interrupted, also getting red in the face. "First, you get those Hinckle brothers turned around and headed back to where they came from. The state police are a different story, so you need to find out who did this thing before they get here, then they'll have nothing to investigate."

Lydia laid into her most condescending tone. "Is that clear enough for you?"

"I had an intimate encounter with a bear last night."

It's not an easy task to shut Pyles and Lydia up but they both suddenly took on silent and confused looks, although Lydia's didn't last long.

She leaned way back, baring her double-going-on-triple chin, and spoke with zero concern. "What the hell's that got to do with anything?"

"The Jenkins lady left a window open." I began tracing the outline of the house on the table-top and pointing out the scenes of action. "Big old bear and two cubs were holed up in the back. Cubs smashed through a pet-door and got out but the mama bear jumped right over me in the living room."

They shared an odd glance. Lydia was about to speak, but I cut her off.

"Most dangerous time to meet up with a bear is a mama with her cubs, they say. But I managed to get that big gal out of the old lady's house and got myself a sniff of her bellybutton for good measure. The bear I mean, not Mrs. Jenkins."

Lydia stiffened in her seat, and the shoddy curtain of propriety that she'd been lurking behind fell to reveal her pure hatred for me. Damn, it felt good.

"Let me tell you—" she started with vehemence.

"Nope! Let me tell you," I interrupted loudly, "that me facing down a four-hundred-pound bear is child's play compared to cleaning up the hit-and-run and getting rid of the Hinckle boys by noon so you all can have your pancake pig-out. But I'll certainly consider your request. And it is a *request* because I don't take orders from either of you."

From the corner of my eye, I saw Sam turning to stifle a laugh at the counter as Lydia exploded, stabbing a finger at the air in front of my face.

"Oh, you'll take charges of malfeasance from us, that's for damn sure! Do your job, Blake. Or someone else will be doing it sooner than you can fuck anything else up!"

"Lydia, please!" Pyles waved his hands before him like he was conducting a mini orchestra on his placemat. "We're not charging anyone with anything. But, Jesus, Blake, how hard can it be to find out who did this? You used to have these things wrapped up in a day."

Staring at the two of them conjured something beyond my wildest imagination as I wished I were in their place instead of mine. It reminded me of being a bleary-eyed, sleepy schoolkid rushing for the door to catch the bus and seeing our cat fast asleep on the couch. Although I didn't want to be a cat, its sweet repose struck me with harsh jealousy, and I ached for such a peaceful state.

"I'm working on it," I mumbled and chugged the rest of my

mug of coffee. "Are we done?"

"You're done," Lydia spat, rifling me a dead stare.

"We want updates throughout the day," Pyles demanded as I stood up and carried the mug back to the counter.

"Then get yourself a scanner," I said over my shoulder. "You can meet me at all the disasters that crop up today. Hell, I'll deputize you, if you want."

Neither of them were paying attention to me anymore, both falling into a hunched-shouldered discussion. Sam had positioned himself at the end of the counter near the door, allowing us a few hushed words of our own.

"I don't know how you put up with those two," Sam whispered, shaking his head.

"It's easy…" I replied and slapped a few bills onto the counter. "I don't. See you at lunch if my appetite comes back."

Pushing open the door, I figured, since I had spent so much time with bears overnight, I might as well poke this one for good measure.

"Hey, Lydia," I called cheerfully, "can you define "malfeasance"?"

"What…? Go do your job!" she blurted.

"It's an act that's illegal and intentional and most often conducted for personal or monetary gain. I've got a few law books in my library if you want to borrow one sometime. But please don't drop by to get it. Send one of your employees whose name you don't even know."

She shouted something else, but the door closing between us saved me from it. Outside in the cold air, the anger and anxiety piling up inside me found their way out, and my hands started shaking and wouldn't stop. I took a bunch of deep breaths and held them for ten seconds, like Tammy had taught me whenever the stress of the job started eating away at my nerves. As soon as I got into the truck and on the road, the yearning to hear from my wife was severe, but I didn't want to put any more calls to her phone as my mind had flipped from thinking like a lawman to a criminal. Calls to her phone were evidence of a coverup that would make it harder to get Cliff off. Building a case for his defense felt almost toxic, and the stomach that had just recently growled for Sam's cooking was in knots while my vision started to blur enough that I pulled the truck over just beyond the edge of town, got out, and rubbed hard at my eyes, waiting for the world to come back together.

Taking a knee on the cold, muddy ground and leaning a hand against a log, I stopped everything from pressing in on me for a couple of minutes. Finally, the dizziness passed and when I stood up, there was only one clear thought that felt true and good.

I can't do this.

A father should never allow his son to get away with murder or manslaughter or whatever they'd pin on Cliff. My kid killed another kid; a nightmare had come alive. I felt a deep, primitive fear reawakening, one that began the day he started preschool, standing with the other parents, watching him out of the corner of my eye as he ran and collided with the other boys on the playground, resisting the strong urge to slow him down or catch him before he fell, allowing the dangerous world to envelope him without my protection. Perhaps warding off my boy's pain and suffering had given Cliff a sense of indestructibility. All the help with schooling, the hours of man-to-man advice, the unconditional love, and the forgiveness, had made a killer out of my son. Rather than casting aside the terrible practices of my own parents, and millions of others before, maybe we should've spanked Cliff or used a belt, like my father did during those confrontational, angry years in high school when boys test the nerves of everyone around them, seemingly for sport. My dad turned any youthful challenges to his authority into a lesson in how to avoid future pain. Could it be that a harsher upbringing would've instilled enough fearful compassion never to leave another human being to die on the side of the road?

The sound of the cell phone buzzing in the truck got me back into the moment, but by the time I jumped into the cab, the call went to messages and the two-way radio crackled to life with

Stacey's voice, sounding tired but concerned.

"Hey, sheriff, you out there? Over."

For a moment, I thought about not answering it. She might say that the state police picked Tammy and Cliff up on the interstate and the car matches our suspect vehicle. At least, their getting caught would bring an end to this ordeal, but I hastily snuffed out the shameful wish by firing up the truck. This nasty business would get taken care of, and on my terms.

My resolve was one thing, but my answer came out anxious and shaky.

"Stacey, it's Blake, what's up?"

"Hey, Sheriff, you in the truck? When do you ever sleep?" Stacey joked before she changed her tone. "So, we just got a call from the state police…"

My hand was on the gearshift, prepared to gun this machine for home but I just squeezed it hard instead, waiting for the verdict.

"They got a 911 signal from a phone somewhere in the North Preserve, Massachusetts area code, probably a hiker, they figure. And pretty near the road, definitely within a mile or so. Over."

I exhaled and let my shoulders ease down from their hunch. "Text me the image of the location."

"Got it. I'll do it right now. and sheriff…" Stacey let her weary words trail off and then blurted, "I heard people talkin' that there's going to be a manhunt for whoever killed that kid? Are you in charge?"

She was serious enough to forget to say 'over'. I got serious, too.

"Stacey, today's going to be one bad fucking day, so do me favor…," I smirked ever so slightly as I kicked the truck into drive. "After your shift, go over to Sully's, get a whole bunch of chips and soda, and go home and sit on your couch and watch TV with your family till you can't stand it anymore. I promise I will envy you for that. Over and out."

I stomped on the gas pedal and flew down the empty country road wishing that I were heading across any state of the union but here. I swore, if there was even a slight chance of a normal life after this shit was over, then I'd pack a duffel bag full of cigarettes, grab my tent, and head for a never-ending camping trip so far north that I could wake up every morning and choose between taking a leak in the US or across the border into Canada.

* * *

The satellite images that Stacey sent weren't very good, looking more like a dark, deep-sea photograph, or blurry sonagram printout. Even without it, I knew where the 911 message had come from as there was only one parking lot in the North Preserve, and the trail into the woods from it doesn't break for over two miles. Hunters never use the lot. Instead, they just pull off and vanish into the wood line at will or whenever they spot a good-sized buck, so the state police were correct in assuming it was a lost or injured hiker. Crazy thing is that a hunter with a gunshot wound—outdoor sportsmen do confuse each other with wildlife on occasion—is far easier to haul in and fix up than some city person who decides to go hiking in the wilderness with no map or water. By the time you reach them it's like trying to calm down a terrified monkey.

Coming out of town, the only vehicle parked off the wood's road was Toby Jeffers' Jeep Cherokee, as he spends most Sunday mornings tracking down birds with his camera. Toby refuses to own a cell phone, so the only call for help that he'd put in is from his own mouth. When I stopped near the hiking trail's parking lot, I checked my phone for any word from Tammy or Cliff but found only a string of hate-texts recently sent by Lydia.

There were three cars in the lot, two next to each other and one on the opposite side. Even before I got out of the truck, the two parked together looked to me like campers, beater cars with bumper stickers from national parks and tons of extra gear stuffed in the back, a mishmash of tarps, ponchos, and sleeping bags. The car on the other side was a newer Audi with a Massachusetts plate and had "young professional seeking adventure" written all over it. Still, a 911 call is somebody's emergency, so I quickly got out, checked the Audi was locked to rule out a stolen vehicle, then set off into the woods to track down yet another lost soul.

The North Preserve is an area of about three thousand acres, cordoned off from the legions of loggers back in the early 20th century by a salt-of-the-earth governor who christened it protected wilderness. Its topography has changed little over the years, with the Osataqua River starting an ocean quest from the Mohawk Lake way up north and flowing through the North Preserve on its ancient path to the Atlantic. Only seasonal hunting is permitted in these parts, but if you've got a rod and tent you are welcome year-round to one great, cheap vacation by the banks of the Osataqua, fishing for salmon that teem the waters from May through October, although not in the legions of long-lost days. Many visitors are hikers, and a half-dozen times a year we pull out an injured one with a busted ankle or twisted knee from taking a tumble off the path, while the rest of the calls for help are from someone who is plain lost because they like to wander the woods thoughtlessly and without a compass.

As soon as I hit the path out of the parking lot into the woods, the quiet and familiar environment allowed me to dig deep into thoughts of my family. First off, I had a vision of transporting us back to simpler times when this untouched preserve was part of a larger virgin continent brimming with the fresh life of an old world. Next, I imagined my angst-ridden wife and child racing along a highway, her hands squeezing the steering wheel while he huddled against the passenger door under a blanket of guilt. There were far worse images fighting their way forward such as Mariel Hinckle, lying alone on her couch, exhausted from the crying and the hate and fear coursing through her body, while her vengeance-seeking brothers draw nearer to town by the moment, preparing to heal hurt with more blood. And the worst image of them all is that of the kid, little Philly, lying in the snow, abandoned there, smashed up and trying hard not to die.

I shook my head to shunt all the bad thoughts aside and moved quicker along the path, concentrating instead on the physical world around me: rocks, trees, the squirrels and their many mates foraging the fresh spring forest floor, anything to keep focused on the job and not personal tragedies.

In countless cases of trying to match shirts with pants, Tammy pointed out that I'm terribly color blind, but the diagnosis means nothing in the woods. Here, the shades of browns and greens have no correlation to fashion. The dirt and the moss and the special look of the aged trunks blend into a unique color that's all the rage from the newts to the coyotes. Who are you wearing? Earth, baby, earth.

I hurried my pace but took time to look up above me at the thick canopy of fir and ash and sweet birch whose needles and leaves covered the path's soft soil. From somewhere way off, a gunshot rang out, punching through the intoxicating wonder of this special place with a fistful of reality. A few birds hiding in the tree branches nearby flew off with a brief mix of tweets and screeches.

"Houston, we got a problem," I muttered and took off on a run toward the shot's direction.

No hunting is allowed on Sundays. It's a law across the county, which keeps the woods fairly empty because it's the only state regulation that folks hold to like gospel. Similar to a seaport community's reverence for its fishermen who brave oceanic dangers to haul back its edible treasures, the hunters in Rock Hollow are de facto tribal elders and relish swapping stories about how stocked their freezers are for the winter with fresh venison or bragging up final scores in the 'Yes, Deer!" contest every October, wherein whoever bags the biggest stag takes home the Antler Trophy. They are a proud, tight bunch who call out and banish anyone who dares poach on the Lord's Day, seen as the height of impropriety.

Now there was potentially a weapon involved, the plans for assisting an injured hiker with their bum ankle had changed to more frantic possibilities like a gunshot wound, loss of blood, and getting a body hastily out to the truck with a fireman's carry. Also, with my shit-rotten luck, there was a decent probability that the hunter might be Keith Griffin, the only bastard who continues to shoot wherever and whenever he pleases because he's a mad-man. His squatter's paradise is just west of the Preserve, and he consistently hunts over the boundaries, not too far but just enough to be a nuisance. Strangely, at the moment, dealing with him again seemed not as bad as everything else on my to-do list.

"Help! Help!"

It sounded like a high-pitched cry of a fox or bobcat at first, but as the words registered, I cut off the path and ran toward it. After another much closer frantic call, a young red-haired girl came bounding through the woods, covered in mud and her face stricken with fear, which only grew when she caught sight of me. She halted and let out a little scream.

"It's OK, it's OK," I said with my palms outward, "I'm the sheriff. I'm here to help."

"Oh, my God," she stammered and ran to me, pulling at my arm. "Please, come on! Michael's there. The man has my boyfriend!"

"OK, we're going," I said grimly, noticing that, under her unzipped fleece jacket, the shirt was pulled open with buttons missing—always a bad sign. "But first you gotta tell me what's happening?"

"I…Jesus, oh…" She was frantic but recovered enough to spit out the situation in between gulping breaths. "We were hiking and…stopped at that old mill… to take pictures…and this guy, this maniac…said we were on his land…he has a gun and he…"

"Come on!"

I grabbed her hand and led her straight off toward Griffin's place, finally letting go when the brush thickened. She fought to keep up with me, her silence providing confirmation we were heading toward her boyfriend. Whipping past prickly bushes and navigating gullies that still held old, stubborn frost took some time but once we held a steady pace, she breathlessly added detail.

"We didn't mean to trespass…hit my boyfriend…grabbed at me…crazy fucking asshole has a gun…"

After a while, she fell back some. I knew the terrain pretty well and pulled ahead, preferring that she stayed hidden while I dealt with the crazy fucking asshole, but soon after I stopped to catch my breath on the shaded grass behind the old paper mill, she jogged up behind, panting hard but still talking.

"House is on the other side…he's crazy."

"Listen," I spoke quickly, "you gotta stay back and let me handle things. I know this nut job and you don't want to be part of whatever's coming. I'll get your boyfriend, don't worry. Just stay back, you hear?"

She nodded and cast her eyes down.

"It'll be alright, trust me." I said as gently as I could and then moved off to face yet another wild animal, knowing full well that trust would never come into play if Keith had been up drinking all night, and he'd sure looked like he was warming up for a bender yesterday.

I made my way with careful haste around the crumbling hulk of the factory and through the muddy expanse that long ago was a parking lot and probably a horse corral in the years before that. Within fifty yards of the shack, another gunshot echoed through the still morning air and killed my plans for a stealth arrival. I drew my weapon and sprinted around the dwelling. In the back, the other hiker was busy digging a deep hole in the ground. Although only his head and the tops of his shoulders were visible, he caught sight of me as soon as I ripped around the corner. Keith was standing nearby with a rifle crooked in his arm and smoking a cigarette which he flicked away as he turned in my direction.

"Sheriff, shiiiiiit…" Keith chuckled to himself but also straightened his rifle and trained it right on me before turning it toward the guy in the hole "I get to tell you to fuck off twice in a weekend? Weeeee! OK, fuck off, Lone Ranger!"

"Put the rifle down, Keith," I spoke with dead seriousness, my weapon drawn and pointed straight at him. "Let the fella go, and then we'll get outta here."

"Nah," Keith replied out of the corner of his mouth, clearly being caught on morning two of a sloppy jag, his tongue heavy, eyes glazed. "I got trespassin' on this motherfucker. Might shoot him as soon as he's done diggin' my well."

He took a few steps closer to the hole, which I was relieved was not meant to be the young man's grave. I moved closer also, but Keith turned the rifle back on me and barked.

"Back off, Sheriff!"

Keith is a man who stays steadily drunk with beer but when the hellion in him rises he adds bottom-shelf whiskey to the mix. Although he appears to be a functioning human, his mind collapses leaving an angry madman. I've made a lifelong rule never to trust the trigger fingers of the insane and perpetually itchy, which is why I had the sudden realization that I'd probably have to shoot this crazy bastard. In my head, I was calculating the odds of a shoulder versus a leg wound.

"You all right, son?" I asked the hiker while keeping eyes trained on Keith.

"H-he…he said he's gonna kill me!" the young man wept. "He tried to…"

"I never said I'd kill him," Keith laughed. "Said I'd shoot him. That's a far cry from—"

"Climb out of that hole now," I demanded as Keith turned fully toward the hiker, allowing me to sneak another few steps.

"Dig, motherfucker!" Keith raged and fired a shot in the air.

The hiker disappeared into the hole with a scream, and I crouched down, ditching the odds of gunshot survival and pointing my pistol straight at Keith's head.

"Drop that fucking rifle!"

"You gonna drop yours?" he drawled, and our eyes locked hard.

"Let him go," I said with gritted teeth, standing up again with my weapon rigid. "Hey, buddy, get out of the hole right now. He ain't gonna hurt you or I'll shoot him dead."

It seemed like the poor guy might have passed out because nothing happened for a moment. Finally, he peeked his head up.

"Go ahead," Keith waved a dismissing hand. He had apparently tired of the game. "Coulda dug that much in my sleep, anyway."

The hiker scrambled out and I got a good look at him, dressed just as fancy as his female companion in high-brand gear, looking like a young runny-nosed kid bawling after being spanked. He kept his eyes on Keith while backing away toward the house.

"Get going," I ordered. "Go find your girl."

"Best keep that piece of ass off my property," Keith called after him. "Next time I'll get diggin' at her hole!"

The hiker scrambled over to the side of the house.

"Fuck you, asshole!" he shouted as he ducked around the corner. I sort of admired him for not fleeing in silence.

"Motherfucker," Keith moved to chase after the guy, and I fired a shot into the air, causing him to whirl on me. "You wanna gun fight, huh?"

"I want to go home and eat breakfast but I'll do it after shooting you, sure enough."

"Those two were trespassin' on my—"

"This ain't your property! You're fucking drunk and crazy!"

"I guess that's what they'll say. Keith Griffin shot the sheriff cause he was crazy."

He took a couple of steps toward me, croaking the Bob Marley song.

"I'll shoot you dead!" I shouted and never had I made such a promise.

"I'll shoot you fuckin' deader!" he growled and moved to take the last step of either his or my life.

"Stop!!"

We both whirled to the source of the high-pitched scream and saw the girl hiker near one of Keith's pickup trucks. She must have rounded the factory on the other side, just missing her boyfriend's escape.

"Get out of here!" I bellowed.

"Where's Micheal?" she replied in the same shaky screech.

"He's long gone, darlin'!" Keith's voice had such an evil edge. "You go on in the house and lay down. I'll be right with you!"

He cackled and drew the gun right back on me.

"Your boyfriend's safe. Go find him and get out!" I shouted and took a few steps to one side so that the sun would get in Keith's eyes a bit more. "Get out! Now!"

The girl scampered away, but Keith couldn't let it go.

"I'm coming after you!" he shrieked. "Here I come!!"

He fired another round into the air. While the girl disappeared fast, I moved even further so that the light would be directly in his sight line. The early spring sun offered just a weak glare, but it was the only means to improve my odds in a bare yard.

"Put it down, Keith!"

"They was on my property. Nobody hangs round my property."

"Lower the weapon, now!"

To my great surprise and relief, he did. Not only did his arm come down, but he dropped the rifle to the ground.

"Why you always bustin' up my romances?" he asked in a singsong voice while retrieving a fifth of liquor from his coat.

"I'm taking you in."

"Nahhhh," he drawled long and slow, the word lingering in his throat before gulping two large slurps from the bottle. "Fuck that shit. You know, I woulda shared that gal with you. Seein' how you shared yours with me."

"I'm calling the Staties. You're going back to jail."

"Your bitch knew you was right out on the porch." He spoke calmly while clumsily fishing a cigarette out of the breast pocket of his soiled flannel shirt. "She didn't care. Damn, son, you must not take care of shit at home. She was all over me like a fuckin' horned-out cat in heat."

I didn't want the switch to snap on inside my head, but it did. I ran at Keith and he got down into a fighting stance, but I still had the gun on him.

"Toss that piece, you dickless fuck!" Keith's eyes blazed with a hatred that I'd never seen before or maybe chose not to. "Toss it! Come on! You pussy! No wonder you got a whore wife!!"

Not that there's any strict code of law enforcement in Rock Hollow, but the one that I steadfastly hold to is to never give up my weapon. Most thieves and killers have a way of talking their way out of situations, and the crazy ones also have the uncanny ability to talk you *into* situations. Add to that a burning hatred, and the sneering devil choosing to taunt me about Tammy at exactly the worst time that anyone could squeeze my nerves, and you had a recipe for disaster fully baked.

The oven door flew open. A mental timer dinged as loudly as a ringside boxing bell, kicking off Buskin vs. Griffin II.

I let the gun drop to the ground and swung hard with a tightly clenched fist, bringing it down on him over and over again while clutching his jacket with the other hand. He probably landed a half-dozen punches on my head, but I didn't feel anything.

The harder my brain got sloshed, the more awful thoughts got cleared away and gas was dumped on my burning rage as I took a savage delight in punching, swearing, spitting out blood until Keith managed to land a vicious kick to my groin, driving a white-hot flash of hurt up my body.

He yanked on me hard and we both tumbled. His eyes were on fire as we hit the ground hard. Rolling to one side, I tried to suck air in to put out the blaze in my gut and drew up on my knees in time to see Keith scrambling in the dirt after my gun.

I leaped for his legs, but he kicked me hard in the face. A blast of stars shot past my eyes, and I fell back on top of something cold and hard. Reaching under for what felt like a crowbar, I pulled out the barrel of Keith's rifle.

He dove for my weapon, pointing and firing a shot that zinged right past my ear. I swung the rifle and pulled the trigger twice. The first shot hit him in the shoulder and the second in the center of his chest, exploding in a spray of blood. Keith staggered backwards, letting out a massive gasp before he crumbled in a puddle of mud. He shuddered for a moment and then nothing.

After staring at his still body and fighting to suck in enough air to slow my pounding heart, the aches from Keith's pummeling set in; a stinging, swollen lip, bad ringing in the ear that took a few fists, and a real sore jaw. On the heels of the pain was a crippling torrent of shame filling me up fast. Fucking stupid drunk asshole! Fuck! The worst part is that the pangs of guilt hammering me weren't because Keith was dead— he had fired first and almost killed me. The fact is part of me wanted him dead. I hated him, even as we both lay here, me frozen with shock but still breathing while his eyes were staring up at nowhere.

There's no undoing this one, Keith. You're fucking cooked. Oh, God-damn it!

The hole opening inside me was some kind of hunter's remorse, made more sickening by the mortal consequences. An urge swelling up; a deep wish that I hadn't taken life again colliding with a refusal to stand up and face the world as a killer, just as dirty as any other, after claiming the prize at the end of a ruthless sport.

I suppose a long time passed before I tried to move again, and when my body finally broke out its temporary freeze, the result was a roll onto my hands and knees so that I could throw up, spitting out a mix of blood from my battered mouth and the bile of a wrenched stomach.

After falling over onto my back, I stared up at the few thin clouds in a pale blue empty sky. The first man I'd killed was a vagrant who'd held up Sully's gas station and pistol-whipped the kid behind the counter unconscious and bloody before taking off into the mountains on foot. I caught up with him that night because the stupid bastard had a big campfire burning like he was on holiday, and the scene went down somewhat like with Keith. He shot first and then I finished him off. But the blinding shine on this one was because of its history, and maybe it's cursed inevitability. At the end of the day, there was no escape from the strange and grasping bond between me and Keith other than one of us killing the other.

"Fuck!" I finally found my voice again, rolling over and beating the ground with each curse. "Bastard! Motherfucker! Fuck, fuck, fuck!!"

It hurt even to stand. My bones and muscles felt like they were seizing up like an old machine ready for the scrap pile, so I smacked and shook my arms and legs like I'd just awoken after sleeping in a bad position. The nightmare kept lying on the ground in front of me, stiff and going cold. When I killed that guy in the woods, I sat by his campfire for a long while thinking about what I'd done and not being OK with it at all. Hell, I could have easily wound up as a landscaper. Plenty of summers in high school, I cut lawns and trimmed hedges for decent cash. Or maybe I could've finished college and moved to the city and sold real estate or something instead of shooting dead other human beings in the woods.

Now, after taking a second life, there was no time for dark meditation or rationalizations of justice. He shouldn't have shot at me. I told Keith that aloud several times as I dragged his body over to the hole that the hiker had been digging and rolled it in, tossing the rifle down after him so that Keith could conduct his next shootout with the devil.

With no time to waste, I shoveled one wild scoop of dirt after another until the hole was almost full, but the soil had lost its compression and there wasn't enough to fill it. Deciding to return and finish the job later, I went into the shack and found some sets of keys, one of which belonged to the Chevy. Its engine sputtered and coughed in resistance to not being warmed up, the entire vehicle vibrating badly as I steered it atop the hastily prepared grave.

"See you in hell, Keith," I muttered after getting out of the truck and tossing the keys a few yards away into a patch of Indian grass.

On the way back, the trail was empty, and the parking lot was missing the car with the out-of-state plates. Still, the two hikers could easily have gone to report the whole scene to the station back in town.

After slipping into the cab of the truck and letting the engine warm up, I pulled out two other items I'd found on the counter next to Keith's car keys. I was soon leaning into the blaze from a black Bic lighter and drawing long and hard on the unfiltered smoke of a dead man's cigarette.

Chapter Four

There was no reason to call the station. If the hikers were already there, reporting the scary episode to a bleary-eyed, overwhelmed Stacey, then the dirty business was blown to shit, anyway. Assuming a defeated, stoical mindset, I said screw it and drove home, purposefully taking the long, winding road outside of town where two mountains intersect, and the big cell tower can't get its blanket of radio waves across it. I'd driven slowly down this long stretch countless times during many text wars with Tammy. The Wi-Fi dead zone allows a quiet retrieval of rational thought from dangerously aggravated heights of anxiety. Everyone should have a place to get the hell away from the buzz of technology so you can realize that being able to chat with your spouse or kids while you're at the farm stand or out on the lake fishing is not life-or-death.

This thinking brought back a memory of Cliff when he was twelve-years old and the major drama of his life was that his friends all had cell phones and he didn't. I longed for the lost days when his pals were jealous of his police scanner and walkie-talkies, which were swiftly replaced by constant chatter, live stream gossip and mean messages via the electronic appendage sprouting from every child's hand at progressively younger ages. Cliff finally sold us with the promise that a phone would help our family communication, hitting me where it hurts by using as a prime example those long stretches of hours when I'm working.

Of course, from the moment he laid his hands on the device, he fell in with the planet of other youngsters across the globe who are complete slaves to their tiny screens. And what did I learn from all that? No matter how high you build a cell tower, it won't ever help family relations a damn if you don't know how to talk to your kids in the first place. Our household had mutated into a prime example of dysfunction, with a father/son team who will run you down or shoot you dead, and the sloppy, adulterous husband and wife. Line up those Ten Commandments in the front yard, folks; the Buskin clan will smash them up one by one. Those trusty words that Moses jotted down while conversing with God began ticking off in my head.

"Thou shalt have no other gods before me."

Well, I'm having a hard enough time being forsaken by just one, so…

"Thou shalt make no idols."

I couldn't come up with anything that humanity has created that was better than what the good Lord had given us to pray to. Beer, maybe.

"Thou shalt not take the name of the Lord in vain."

He must have put that one in just to be sure we'd stay sinning plenty when smashing a thumb with a hammer or stubbing a toe in the dark, a law that wouldn't be a law unless broken repeatedly.

"Thou shalt not…"

It finally struck me as unhealthy thinking and the words scattered as I rubbed a couple of fingers to my eyes. Obviously, "Thou Shalt Not Kill" was waiting there at number VI or VII, my days of religious studies leaving mostly confusion, like the rest of junior high. Its dire warning was lurking up ahead somewhere, like an ash and brimstone-stained conductor ready to punch tickets for Cliff and myself on a one-way train to the underworld.

"Jesus Christ," I muttered, adding another dose of forever to my fiery afterlife, "I gotta get some sleep."

Instead, I smoked two more of Keith's cigarettes during the ride, tossing the second out the window and onto my driveway as I pulled in, welcoming the guilty yet positive sensation that we might have bought a little more time. That's why we got rid of the car. No way were we going to make this right, but somehow I figured if we put our heads together maybe we could…could what? Be a family for a little while? This was what it took for us to recognize each other as all we had in the world?

There was deep irony in finding Tammy's Subaru gone, bringing me back to the many mornings before dawn when I'd finally returned home from a twelve-hour shift and my headlights would cross the empty space of blue gravel laid down specially so she wouldn't get stuck during snowy, frozen winters. The car's absence always preceded a note on the kitchen table that she'd left, not saying for how long, and no words of remorse for the motherless child in bed, followed by a pint of whiskey sloshing in my belly before sunup. This time, at least, the missing car brought a flash of pleasure as my wife had somehow followed my advice for once. The pressure in my aching head eased up a touch and brought on a sudden, heavy urge to sleep, even just for a few minutes, but the damned duty of the job nagged at me enough to pick up the handset and call Stacey.

"Stacey, it's Blake."

The air crackled and buzzed for long enough to signify that she'd been napping, which was heartening. I'll take any kind of peace as a good sign.

"Hey," came the mumble, "sorry, Sheriff, I was…Did you get to whoever it was in the woods?"

"Yup," I replied and let my eyes flow along the contours of my yard, the familiar hedges and brownish-green spread of grass interspersed with lawn games, left out over the winter: corn-hole and horseshoes. The whole picture brought a sting of pain to my heart as the lying began.

"It was a couple of lost hikers…on drugs, I guess. All whacked out. They ran off. Let me know if they show up in town."

"Drugs? What kind of drugs? Over," inquired Stacey, now awake with teeming curiosity.

"Never mind. I'm home. Need to sleep for an hour, and then I'll be in."

"Hey did you—"

She was about to let loose with a torrent of questions yet was likely not surprised when I begged off the call. The 911 report still had to be closed with the state police, but since they were in no hurry to help me out with the Hinckle brothers, those guys could play the waiting game themselves. Fact was that every damn thing in the world could fuck off until I ate something and laid down for long enough to get my head into some kind of order.

Once up the back steps and into the kitchen, the first stop was the Fig Newtons. Tammy cut off bringing treats home when things went south with us— a nod to the end of the pleasures life had once bestowed upon me, so I grab a big package whenever I'm at the market. My custom is to knock back about a dozen of them with two glasses of milk, but this time I just chewed through and swallowed at least that many while standing at the kitchen table, finally bending to wash them down with gulps of cold water from the faucet.

"Hey."

Instinctively, my knees dropped to the floor, and I jerked around with my weapon out of its holster.

"Jesus, Dad!

Cliff's face was barely visible beneath the black hoodie, but the familiar thick shock of brown hair jutting out at the fringe disarmed me instantly.

"Don't sneak up on me!" I barked, standing and holstering the gun.

"I'm sorry," Cliff snapped right back, yet in a quieter voice, "I thought you were Mum. What the hell happened to you?"

I'd forgotten the whacks from the fight with Keith and turned to the sink to rub a squirt of dish soap and splash some handfuls of water across my face.

"I had a run-in with a hiker, and it got ugly," I mumbled through a small towel pressed hard to my smarting mouth and cheeks. "When did Mum leave?"

"I don't know. Middle of the night," Cliff replied, always an easy bean-spiller. "She said to stay here until she calls."

"So, keep on doing that. I need to lie down."

Moving to the couch in the living room was like walking through sand. Something kept pulling at me to get out there and solve the crisis, but there was no escaping complete exhaustion, and soon I was lying deep among pillows and a musty-smelling blanket.

"What's gonna happen to me?"

It's possible that I slept for a minute because when I opened my eyes, Cliff was on the big brown easy chair across the room, sitting straight up and not looking at all easy.

"Just let…" I was about to beg him to let me rest, but when he's really upset, his face reminds me of him as a little guy. "I'm trying to take care of things, bud. It's a big mess."

"I don't want to go to jail." He was trying to hold it together, but the next words came out with a slight whimper. "I can't."

I sat up and looked squarely at him through the slight, sleepy blur. "Kid, you killed somebody."

He didn't respond and instead sank deeper inside the hoodie until only his eyes and nose were visible. This usually annoys the hell out of me. Often, I'd explain that when I see teens his age out there ducking around with their hoods pulled tight around their heads, particularly when it's warm weather, it tells me they're up to something. In his favor, exhaustion had me in a chokehold and for the moment I just stared at the big bookcase holding my LP records, treasures collected from back rooms and basements of music stores in Portland and occasionally Boston, relics of golden days whenever a free high school weekend would coincide with extra cash for train fares and low budget purchases of classic vinyl. Shit, I could use a blast of The Who or Deep Purple because I had zero power left in my battery. Still, I can always tell when the boy is scared, and the prickly guilt of fatherhood will never let me sleep.

"You're eighteen…and you've never been in trouble." Now I sounded like I was building a case for his defense.

"Not that anyone found out about," Cliff mumbled and slowly lifted his head out of the hood like a turtle searching for flies, "right?"

A truly disturbing landmark in parenting is when your child grows up and learns how to cut you to shreds, leaving your mouth agape in silence. This utter stupefaction rivals the first moment of discovering what a toxic and choking mix of waste a cute little infant will leave in the diaper for you to clean up. Both experiences are shocking, somewhat repulsive, and tolerated with steadfast patience and shallow breathing.

Cliff's latest attempt to take me out at the knees referred to a bad night last summer when he and some friends got locked up by some boondock cops while camping upstate. Turned out, a friend of a friend got invited along and got rip-roaring drunk not long after pitching his tent. At some point in the night, after arguing about noise with a husband and wife at a nearby campsite, he went to his truck and collected a chainsaw and set about terrorizing the couple for twenty minutes. After the saw's gas ran out, the traumatized campers fled and retrieved the nearest town's police who hauled Cliff and his cohorts to the station, resulting in the chainsaw guy getting booked for aggravated assault, and the rest of the dummies for underage drinking and a bag of weed. No other parents got there before me. After a private chat with the arresting officer, Cliff got let off with a warning never to come back to that stretch of the state in exchange for cleaning up the tents and gear that the cops had strewn about the site. We never talked much about it afterwards, and I had stored it away in the back of my mind as just a bad episode in an otherwise good kid's life.

"So, you're saying my getting you off that time upstate led to you killing somebody?"

"It was an accident!" he shouted, jerking his body in the chair. "Nobody tried to kill anyone! It was an accident!"

"When you hit the kid, it was an accident. When you left him there, that's…Why, Cliff? Why didn't you tell me? I could've—"

"This isn't fair!" He jumped up and stomped out of the room.

When he slammed his hands on the kitchen counter, I figured the kid needed a dose of reality instead of being allowed to rage against the judgements of the universe.

"Cliff! Stop!" I demanded as I stumbled into the kitchen, my legs apparently trying to sleep without the rest of my body.

He obliged by covering his face with his hands, although the expected sobs didn't come. He stopped crying in front of me a few years ago, moving into another room or going outside when he needed a good wail, like any healthy teenager should do. I didn't notice until Tammy pointed it out. By then, I felt it would embarrass him if I brought it up.

"You need to know what kind of trouble is brewing over this. Mariel Hinckle's brothers are coming, probably already here. They want to hunt down whoever did this."

"What?" He dropped his hands, and the rage fell away, leaving only confusion as he asked with a tremble, "What do I do? Can't you help me?"

I assured him but not with something he wanted to hear. "Yes. If I bring you in, we can have you transferred over to the state police barracks by…"

"You *are* going to arrest me! What the fuck, Dad!"

"Listen—"

He glared with what I hoped wasn't hatred. "No. No! Go away. Get the hell out of here! Just…just pretend I wasn't here. Give me an hour, and you'll never see me again."

"You're talking crazy, kid," I pleaded. "Where will you go? You going to drop out of school?"

"Yeh, Dad! If you send me to jail, I will have to drop out of school! What the fuck? What the *fuck*!"

He started pacing around the room, pulling at his hair, and slapping my hand away when I reached toward him.

"Mum said you would fix this. She promised! But I knew you wouldn't. Cause you don't give a shit about us!"

"I want to protect you in the best way I can." To my dismay the tears had fought their way into my eyes. "I only ever want to keep you safe. This is killing me, too!"

"Let me go. Tell them you don't know where I am."

"I can't…"

"Dad," he pleaded and drew near, searching for my eyes, which I kept averted, "I swear to you, I'm not bad. I'm not. This was an accident that was nobody's fault. And just because…just because you hate Mumma doesn't mean you have to hate me, too."

"Cliff…"

"You never talk to me anymore except to tell me how I fuck everything up. You're never here. We used to hang out all the time. We used to…be best friends!"

He couldn't keep the tears back any longer, collapsing his head into his arms on the granite counter of the island, cluttered with mail, keys and other shit. I couldn't hold back anything either.

"Cliffy," I cried, and this time he let me put a hand on his shoulder, "I'm sorry this family fell apart. I'm so sorry. And I am your friend, kid. I am. I want to help you."

He lifted his red, tear-strewn face to me. "Then do it…please."

"Tell me exactly what happened."

His body went rigid. "I don't want to."

"Buddy, you're gonna have to tell…"

He backed off the counter and yanked away from me.

"I don't have to say anything! This…it wasn't my fault!!"

Cliff tore out of the kitchen and hit the stairs, his steps pounding up to his room. After the slamming door and his body hitting the bed, his muffled sobs filtered through the floor and went straight through me down here, long and desperate and each one deeper than the last. Many times, during his childhood, when we all innocently mount good old rage for a ride, he had lost his shit plenty and cried himself hoarse, mostly in the early years, but every so often we'd gotten a teenage outburst, or as Tammy called it, an "emotional release."

Every time, and never more than this moment, those howls remind me what a rotten dad I am, such a terrible card for a kid to draw in life. I couldn't even go up there and tell him that I'd save him, or that there was nothing to be afraid of, because there were a shit-ton of things to fear today. A father's primary duty is to set an example for a young man to survive in this world. Comfort has no place— it's mainly grit that gets you anywhere. But heading to prison at eighteen is not a survival lesson; it's three strikes in one pitch. He wouldn't get out in four or five or maybe even ten years and be ready to hit the books at college. It would truly break him, and I'd be the one sending him to hell. Why couldn't I stop being a horrible fucking father?

After Cliff had quieted, I walked around the house for a few minutes, noting all the things that I'd never found time to fix like a slow leak in the bathroom faucet, cracked window in the laundry room, window screens grimy with dust and lint and dead bugs from expired summers, and everything sorely in need of a fresh coat of paint. The walls were decorated with tons of photos of Cliff; his face everywhere around the house in dozens of framed pictures. At the age of six, laughing hysterically on the edge of a frozen creek, or suiting up at fourteen for his first high school baseball game, or looking away from the camera except for one mischievous eye lit up like a devil's disciple, or a real sweet smile by sixteen flickering candles on a birthday cake. Images stuck in time of a happy little boy and a smolderingly handsome young man greeted me in every room.

By the time I had moved through the entire downstairs, spending tortuous moments at each picture, there was no other choice left to me. I somehow had to save my son from drowning in danger. Once back in the kitchen, I picked up my phone and dialed.

Stacey answered after one ring. "Hey, Sheriff. I thought you were gonna get some sleep?

"No time. Listen, I need you to get together a warrant."

"Is it about the Hinckle boy? You got somebody?" She sounded ready to fly through the phone.

"Yeh," I exhaled, "I think so."

"Who is it?"

Cliff's senior yearbook photo had recently arrived in the mail, and Tammy had stuck all different sizes up on the refrigerator with those stupid magnets she collects from hick town shops. That face, though, that face. Everybody says he looks like his mother, and maybe that's why it hurts inside whenever he smiles at me. Hell, even though it's broken and hardly works right, the only kind of love I've ever known has come from those two.

"Keith Griffin," I said coldly, "I'm going out to his place right now to get him."

"Figures, right?" she replied in distaste. "Tears around town like a drunk maniac. It just figures."

"Right."

"I swear, too many bad people in this world."

"Don't I know it."

I skipped the goodbye and hung up, then opened the refrigerator and chugged down a half quart of orange juice before heading upstairs to Cliff's room. When I pushed the door open after a cursory knock, he turned over on the bed and clutched at two pillows. I stepped in and gazed out the window.

"I want you to stay put. Let me talk to Mum and maybe you two don't have to go anywhere."

He was a mess of confusion, but there was hope in his eyes. "What about the accident?"

"Maybe it's time you start telling yourself that someone else did it." I kneeled down by the bed, my stomach gnawing itself hollow.

"How do…you know?" His eyes grew big and he sort of flinched away from me.

"Think of it like you had a bad dream. Then you woke up and found out that you didn't do it."

He stared at me, silent and brooding. We probably would've stayed like that for a long time, but not on this particular Sunday.

"I didn't do it," he whispered.

"That's right," I grunted, standing and finding it hard to balance for a split-second. "Somebody else did it. I got work to do, and in the meantime that's all you have to tell yourself. You didn't do it."

"I didn't do it," he said a bit louder.

"OK. I gotta go. If you talk to your mum first, tell her to call me. Got it?"

Cliff nodded his head and sat up a little.

"Dad?"

"Yeah?"

"Thank you."

"No thanks here, kid." I looked him squarely in the eye, like one man to another. "There's a big, bad line we're crossing over today. But at least we're crossing over as a family."

He stared down at the rumpled brown blanket around his legs and didn't look up again. I closed his door behind me and went downstairs to grab my other revolver and extra shells.

Standing in the hallway with the front door half-open, I felt the old life of the house rushing out into the chill of the morning. All the good times, as few as they were, and even the making-up periods after bad times with their tender sorrow, pouring out fast, light as air and just as irretrievable. With no chance of bringing any of it back, I stepped outside and slammed the door tight behind, wishing hard to keep anything else from escaping and being lost forever.

Chapter Five

There wasn't much foot traffic in town when I pulled up to the station. A number of folks were parking cars outside or heading into the church to join the rest of the congregation for services, giving me about a half-hour, or forty-five minutes if Father Drake got lost in his sermon. Just about enough time to get up to Keith's place and take care of the body before I'd have to get back here and wait for the day to really get wild. Due to his imminent warrant, Keith would have to come back out of the ground and disappear forever, because after news spreads of his being the prime suspect in the hit-and-run and suddenly vanishing like a ghost, the old shack by the mill would eventually turn into legend for teens looking to spook themselves at night or local true-crime fanatics poking around during the day.

Sorry, Keith, you'd gotten a few hours of rest in the cold ground, but it was time to sleep with the fish. I hadn't thought it out entirely but the best and quickest plan was to dig him up, damn him to hell one more time, wrap his body in a tarp, then dump it in the deepest drop by the river's edge. Tie some rocks to it, a cinder block would be better. Maybe clear the shack of his wallet or any other important items to give the appearance of his having skipped town. As soon as he made his watery exit, I planned to get the warrant filed and hustled over to the judge for signature, and if he puts up any resistance then I'd mention some really twisted shit tucked away in my back files regarding one of Judge Prowse's whorehouse excursions up north going strangely awry, and *strangely* is hardly the word. Let's just say I saved his bare-assed bacon and he owed me at least one, and the favor was about to be called in.

With Keith Griffin named as Enemy Number One, a big fat phantom grouse would be let loose for the Hinckle brothers to chase around until they grew tired of coming up empty and got to slinking back to the holes that they'd crawled from, leaving a few state lines between us.

"Who punched you in the face?" Stacey asked, her eyes widening the moment I walked into the station.

She was a smaller gal who added to her height with a huge poof of brown hair held up by the same invisible force that keeps the whole office smelling like a beauty salon. Great dispatcher, hell of a stink.

"The hiker," I lied too easily. "Must've been high as a kite."

"I hope you returned the favor." she said as she handed over the paperwork, still warm from the printer. "There you go. No big surprise. Keith Griffin is an asshole."

"With a capital 'A'." I glanced at his name on the warrant, swallowing hard on the foul taste of deceit. "Listen, keep a lid on this right now, 'kay? Don't need the whole town hunting him down. I'm going to search round those woods again to make sure the druggy hikers are gone for good. Then I'll go looking for Griffin."

After all these years of sniffing out liars and degenerates, the black arts of their trade were becoming way too easy to perform. The parallel outward slick talk and internal plotting of dirty deeds began taking over my consciousness, as if my time as sheriff was merely training for the rest of my life as a scheming outlaw. The badge that had grounded me like a charging station for my spirit's battery now felt as if I shouldn't carry it at all. Better to exchange the tin star for a baseball cap pulled way down over the eyes and answering to a different alias in every new town.

In its way, desperation certainly simplifies matters. Drastic life choices are made in a short time, like a player reading a Monopoly card that either plunges the luckless into poverty or showers fortunate fools with temporary wealth and happiness. When things finally go belly-up for good— money gone, real estate lost, reputation in tatters—that's when you tip the board over like a frustrated six-year-old and start all over again. And that's what my family was headed for— a total reboot to square one or…

Go directly to jail. Do not pass go. Do not collect jack shit.

"Did you get their plates? I can run 'em right up."

"No, must've parked off the road," I muttered.

Stacey looked at me, barely holding back a gentle ribbing that could voice her disbelief. We both knew a deer couldn't wag its tail thirty yards off into the woods from any road in our district without my spotting it. I felt her eyes heating up the back of my head as I went to my desk at the far wall of the station where a line of industrial dryers once blew their guts out for fifteen hours a day. Despite deep cleaning with enough bleach to whiten the night, the acrid odor of burned lint persisted long after the machines had been removed. Tammy had tried to fire up all sorts of incense to cut the smell, but the place stank so much of thyme and eucalyptus that I lied and said it had done the trick.

A few moments after sitting down and picking up the phone, I filled the back of the station with cigarette smoke. The old taste was returning after my sucking down one after the other. Cradling the receiver between shoulder and ear, I shot a stern look at Stacey, who had been creeping closer to overhear the call, and she leaped behind her own desk, pretending to be busy.

"State Police Barracks, Troop F," a cold, hard voice greeted me.

At least the smarmy shit from yesterday was pulling other duty. I reached over to grab a half-empty soda can for a make-shift ashtray.

"Hey. This is Sheriff Buskin down in Rock Hollow. We got a 911 call from you guys this morning, but it's since been resolved."

"What town?"

"Rock Hollow," I repeated and took a deep drag of smoke.

"Wherever that is…" The monotone voice now sounded like the prick cousin of the other wise-ass dispatcher.

Ignoring the dig, I went on forcefully. "Right, listen. You can close that 911 call out. And, also, can you send a message up the ladder for me?"

"A message from Rock Hollow." The voice took on a slight humor. Nice to know I could brighten someone's day.

"We have an open hit-and-run death investigation and we got word that some patrolmen might be heading here today. It would be great to get some kind of ETA."

"It *would* be great," he replied and then fell back into robot-mode. "I will close out the 911 and your message is received. Someone will call you."

"OK, thanks."

Shockingly, he hung up without wishing me well in all that I do. After dropping the cigarette into the can with a satisfying sizzle, I grabbed my extra coat and muck boots in case the job at Keith's got sloppy. When I turned around, Stacey was standing near me.

"Sheriff," she said kindly, "are you OK?"

Stacey had a look of concern in her deep brown, almost black, eyes and for a moment it struck me how young she was. Not near Cliff's age but close enough to have no idea what kind of shit life could mire you in.

"Yes," I chuckled. "Why? Did I fuck something up?"

"No, no." She turned away and moved over to the coffee pot on the shelf behind her desk. "It's just…I mean you ain't smoked in forever and…I think you ought to get some deputies on board today."

My impulse was to give curt instructions on how to keep her nose out of official business, but I found her concern sort of nice.

"Appreciate it, Stacey. But I don't need anybody slowing me down. Just keep alert around here, OK? And tell Barbara the same thing. I expect I'll be out most of the day."

"For sure. Barbara's running late so I'll hang out until she's had coffee. She's shit for the first hour, you know."

"I know." I pulled a black ski hat out of the jacket pocket that I wear in cold weather, big yellow letters blaring *SHERIFF* on its brim, and put it on. It wasn't exactly uniform standard but at this point neither am I. "Just like my truck. Hard to get warmed up but steady as shit all day long."

"Yeah!" Stacey laughed. "We'll be on the ball today. You too, sheriff, OK?"

"24/7." I said in farewell, trying to smile but failing miserably and instead stepping out the door.

Moving to my truck, the urge to hustle and gain back precious time lost jolted my legs into action, but since there were a couple more cars parked by the diner and a few more folks out on the sidewalks, I kept it to a respectable but quick shuffle.

I avoided driving down Main Street, where there are too many stop signs and everybody dawdles and clogs up the thoroughfare, townsfolk lassoing each other into hasty gossip with frantic waves from the sidewalk and out of rolled down car windows. Instead, I steered toward the east side of town and passed by the church, surprised and perhaps envious of the considerable number of cars parked in the lot as that's just the place for a transgressor like me right now. What I wouldn't have given to take part in a quiet, meditative mass with nothing else to do but listen, stand, and kneel in the warm confines of St. Peter's, or even the reformed Disciples of Christ over in Marbleton. Hell, I'd even sit crisscross with the new age outfit up in Greenwood who supposedly grow tons of pot in between prayer services. The Almighty is both divine empresario, staging the longest-running production in every flavor of church on earth, and harsh universal critic, for whom we perform weekly, so that He can collect the award for Best Being year in, year out in his omniscient, silent and powerful way. I've never witnessed another event besides church that gets people up early on a Sunday, especially the bitter cold ones. Nothing cultural can match it. Not even a double bill of the Beatles and the Rolling Stones back in their ass-kicking days could do it every week, year, decade, on and on. Eventually everything gets old. Except for the Creator, with apologies to Jagger or McCartney zealots, and his bottomless bag of tricks called faith, it's always there, rock-steady and accessible, being practiced in a church near you. Of course, ready-made salvation can only work if your dirty little soul takes a shine to it or not.

A few blocks past the church, under the cover of the dogwood trees lining the sidewalk, someone was walking at a brisk pace. When my truck came near, it turned out to be a woman suited to the nines in a tight black dress, big heels, and a fur stole, probably fake but fancy enough for this town. She was also covering her mouth with both hands, and I was afraid she was going to be sick, so I slowed down. It turned out she wasn't ill but crying. Finally, pulling up alongside the curb at a break between trees, I discovered that the woman in distress was Mariel Hinckle.

"Hey, Mariel," I called after sliding the passenger window down, but she paid no attention to me. "You OK?"

She turned her face in my direction, revealing a portrait of deep, sad exhaustion. A runoff of tears had thwarted the day's make-up, streaks of mascara still visible on her cheeks, and bags hung under her always bright blue eyes. Even after noticing me, Mariel just kept walking and crying, so I parked, got out and caught up to her on the sidewalk.

"Mariel, hold on."

I was a step behind her when she halted, turned, and fell into my arms, sobbing hard against my shoulder. Taking a side of my unzipped coat, I covered her a bit while she let out a good wave of sorrow, so much that it stoked my guilt and almost caused me to say something stupid. I choked it down and let her pull it together, which she did fairly well before taking a step back.

"I'm sorry, Blake. I…" she said between deep breaths, "I've been so fuckin' angry ever since…So I figured, let's try church. But even with all those people, it was so…empty, cause Philly always went with me."

Mariel set into crying again and offered no resistance as I guided her slowly over to the truck, where she got in without a word. By the time I climbed behind the wheel, she was fishing tissues out of her bag to blow her nose and had begun damage control on the mascara.

"Jesus Christ, I'm a fuckin' mess," she muttered, snapping shut the compact mirror in her hand and shoving it back into her handbag. She gave a quick glance at me. "You don't look so good yourself."

"Cut myself shaving. Let's get you home."

She nodded and pulled the seatbelt on while letting out the deepest of sighs. After plunging her hand back into the bag, she came out with a large pair of sunglasses and donned them before sitting back and tightening the fur around her.

"Oh, I'm a wreck," she muttered.

"Nah, not you." I kept my voice reassuring, despite my conscience raising a big red flag about hanging out with her. "You could roll around in the mud and still come up looking good."

She didn't say anything, so I continued,

"Not a bad idea, going to church. Never was one for it much myself. My dad used to make me go. I suppose it got all mixed up with him. You know, he was—"

"The children kept starin'," she whispered, the tremble of sorrow again quaking beneath her voice. "Parents know enough not to but…the kids…lookin' back with their sad little eyes. And then the stupid priest and his stupid sermon…"

She broke down again, so I put a hand on her shoulder. Mariel's house was only about eight blocks away from the church, and after I eased the car to a stop at her driveway, she calmed down somewhat.

After a few more moments of awkward silence, she turned to me with a hand on the door.

"You look pretty damn tired, Blake. You want some coffee?"

The out-of-the-blue invitation hung in the air. I was struck dumb at the mere thought of sitting down for coffee with a person who ranks in the top five people in the world I needed to steer clear of, like a big old raging bonfire of wrong. Instead of the myriad of other places that I was late getting to, or things that I was desperate to get done, what leaped off the tip of my tongue came out decisively.

"Sure."

I'm just going to blame it on the worsening fatigue, or slow onset of shock, or maybe some kind of mystical snake of fate that's got its coils wrapped around my head, forcing the wrong words to escape my mouth with no real inclination to stop them.

Mariel got out quickly, but a long few seconds passed before I set aside the urge to flee and resignedly shut off the motor. Looking around the hit-or-miss neighborhood as I got out, it became instantly clear that the Hinckle house was the prize of the patch. Exterior in good order, gutters are a little grimy but nice looking and sturdy, clean yard except for some stray balls and a frisbee. Most of the other houses were far less kempt, with ancient paint jobs, way overgrown lawns, tipped and broken chairs at front lawn firepits, and the occasional all-season couch offering guests ample yet damp and moldy seating. To underscore the impression, on the sidewalk a few houses away, a fat guy dressed in sweatpants and a puffer jacket stood holding a leash in one hand and hauling huge drags from a vape pen in the other as his dog urinated at the base of an overflowing trash barrel. Ain't that America.

"When is Tim coming back?" I inquired as she struggled with the keys at the door, finally popping the lock and bumping it open.

"Oh, Jesus," she groaned, "don't get me started."

I knew Tim Adams better than I knew Mariel. We used to play on the town softball team before I tore my knee up and had to retire and sit with the beer-cooler bunch in the stands. About ten years younger than me, not smart but bright enough to fix cars and make a living out of it, Tim was a longtime National Guard member. From what I heard, he was a good soldier, proud of his country, a decent family-man and seemingly an All-American guy, until out of nowhere he got sent to South Korea. Strangely, his guard unit did not get shipped out, just him. Some folks tried to get up a rumor that old Tim had some kind of talent at working on top-secret jet engines until the real story came out. All-American Tim had grown so sick and tired of family life that he chose what to him was an honorable way to avoid simply picking up and disappearing. This way, the army allowed him a graceful exit while his family got their bills paid but nothing much else fulfilled. A despicable and fucked up thing for a man to do to his flesh and blood, but I expect everybody else seems fucked up and despicable to a man like Tim Adams.

"He's not coming?" I asked off-handedly, but it came out wrong.

"You're gettin' me started," she warned and shot me a look, a little more playful than sinister.

"That's shitty. I'm sorry, Mariel. But…what about your brothers?"

"I wondered how long it would take you to get around to them. Pretty honorable. Figured you woulda asked in the truck."

She turned and went into the kitchen and I stepped around the mild clutter of the Hinckle home, jackets, scarves, and boots strewn about, and baskets of unfolded laundry, a common sight in my house. The tables, however, were loaded with an assortment of plastic-wrapped plates, platters, and Tupperware bowls full of baked goods brought by neighbors and loved ones after the accident. I imagined the fridge must be stuffed with trays of lasagna and manicotti, and curiously my appetite came back. I resisted the temptation to slip a cookie from the nearest plate and instead stared out a window, which overlooked the moldy gray siding of the neighbor's house. This stretch of homes was owned by Dan Robinson or Chuck Brennan, and I swore the next time I see either, they'd get dressed down for squeezing these tenants like a couple of slumlords, because that's exactly what they are. Folks in these houses can barely make rent each month after keeping themselves fed, clothed, and healthy, and the least the owners can do is slap a coat of paint on the places occasionally. Stir up some fucking pride, goddamn it.

In the kitchen, the clank of mugs and pouring liquid led to Mariel returning to hand me a warm cup of coffee and inviting us both to sit. She eased into an old cherry wood rocker, kicking off her heels and pushing the chair back with her dark, panty-hosed feet. Her black dress tightened around the waist, and although I had sort of noticed before, the curves currently on display prove without question that she is one hell of a well-built woman. This set off another series of "get-the-fuck-out-here" alarm bells clanging in my noggin, so I chugged the coffee down in two gulps while she gave a bit more detail on her and Tim.

"I really don't fuckin' care. He acted like he wasn't even here long before he left…Maybe he was always like that, I don't know. Even when he's sittin' right next to you, he's a million miles away. Not that I saw much beyond bein' a wife. That's the prize for a poor hick town girl, right? I found me a half-way decent unmarried man with no kids! Jackpot! So, we hurry and get hitched, and only then do we start gettin' to know each other like...like…"

Mariel pushed hard at the coffee table with the bottom of her foot, giving me a start. When she spoke again, the pissed-off wife had taken the place of the grieving mother.

"Fuckin' piece of shit! I mean, you can't at least come back to bury your child? If you can't find it in you to do that then you ain't attached to anythin' in the world, really. You just…ain't no man at all."

She slid aside a mess of unopened mail on the coffee table, placed the cup down, and buried her face in her hands. The comfort of home allowed her to let out a slow, pained moan followed by a stretched-out cry, leaning down and only sitting up a bit when gasping for breath, before even harder sobs overcame her. The family staying with her yesterday had obviously gone, otherwise they would've run to tend to the poor gal's breakdown, a duty which now fell on me.

I kneeled near her chair and unclasped the hands that she'd been wringing hard and held one tight.

"It's OK. Get out whatever you got in there, kid."

"It's that fuckin' priest." She shuddered as she spoke and then looked up to the heavens. "Sorry, God. It's just, you know how Father Drake has been sick, so they have this other guy, Father Coogan, fillin' in…"

"I haven't been keeping up..."

"Well anyway, this guy Coogan is all right. Somebody said they saw him shit-faced at the gas station buyin' cigars, but whatever. So today, mass is goin' OK. I told you the kids were all lookin' at me and that was horrible, but the readin's were really nice, and the gospel was about that blind man Lazarus, who Jesus made see again. I love the ones about Jesus havin' superpowers. But then this Father Coogan gets up for his sermon and I'm all ready for a nice blind-man-gets-his-sight-back story, but this guy starts talkin' about the Book of Genesis!"

"How dare he?"

"Exactly!" Mariel's eyes widened. "I'm the first one to admit that I don't know nothin' about too much but I know my Bible. If the readin's and gospel are from the New Testament, then stick to it! But here goes old fill-in Father Coogan talkin' about Adam and Eve, and the garden and the serpent, and then I swear he starts lookin' my way and sayin' all kinds of shit about the end of innocence bein' part of life; that for us to be human then innocence must be...taken from us to...to..."

She let go and put a hand on my forearm, leaning into it hard. With a fresh round of sobs, she threw herself against me and nearly tipped us both onto the carpet. Steadying us on the rocker and putting one hand lightly to the side of her head, I went for more soothing reassurance but found that my throat was getting tight and the words came out shaky.

"He was...a good kid, Mariel. You're a good mom. All our families have some kind of rot inside of them. Hell, I don't know my wife any better than you know Tim. We just got together and sort of...clung to each other, right? You're a good woman. You're a beautiful girl."

The last words seemed to shock her. She pulled back slightly, and our eyes met in a cross-glance. My attempt at a profuse apology got cut off with a forced, clumsy, yet full-on kiss on the lips from Mariel. Once again, my better self was nowhere to be found, and I kissed her back until we both seemed to jerk away at the same time.

"Jesus," she exclaimed, standing up and grabbing the coffee mug before stepping around me, "what the hell is wrong with me!"

"No, I'm sorry. I didn't mean—"

"Now don't start apologizin'." Mariel laughed nervously, although a frantic look was beginning to appear. "That'll just fuck it up more. You should go. Jesus!"

"Yup. I will. I am." I stammered the words, but my legs moved fast enough toward the front door. "I'm sorry for everything. I really am."

"Just stop apologizin', please? It never helps. Your fuckin' kid gets run down and bleeds to death in the snow, and all the people comin' up and apologizin' is gettin' so…so disgustin'!"

She was pressing the coffee mug to her temple and leaning against the doorway to the kitchen. I left it at that and opened the front door, not looking back because, as terrible as it sounds, that was one heck of a kiss.

"Hey, Blake!"

I caught the door before it closed behind me and turned on the porch to peek through its wide crack into the house.

"My brothers said they'd leave by four in the mornin', figure they'll get here round noon. I'm tellin' you, Blake, just stay out of their way. Somebody out there deserves what they're gonna give 'em."

"I could explain the law to you, if you want…" I tried to be square with her to no avail, and she looked at me like I was speaking in tongues. "But I suspect you'd think it's a crock of shit. All I will say is that they're not helping get past this bad time by looking for revenge. Trust me, Mariel, nothing ever gets better with more blood."

"Bullshit. Go back to church and tell that dumb-ass priest Coogan to teach you some Old Testament. Book of Exodus. An eye for a fuckin' eye. Now, get out. And just…be careful around my brothers, all right? They're dangerous." She gave me one last angry, sorrowful look. "And you best believe I'll be tellin' them the same thing about you."

* * *

In a guilty hurry, I cut back through town. Church services were just letting out, and folks teemed the sidewalks in route for tables heaped with plates of bacon, eggs, and fresh doughnuts, with newspapers and naps to follow. When I took a corner sharply, my truck tearing past as if it were gaining pole position in a stock-car race shocked some of those standing at the corner in conversation. I'd seen the pack coming down the sidewalk, but I had no time and zero interest in conversation with these congregants, fresh from confessing their sins and primed for new gossip, so the stop sign was merely a suggestion. Perhaps it served them all well. Spotting a dangerous sinner is instant reward for the pious and freshly scrubbed soul. At the next corner, the congregation waiting to cross over to the parking lot on the other side of the street wore frowns at my expense, but a few waved as I gave a quick beep while executing the turn. Within the crowd on the way to their cars was Melvin Pyles, and he wore the biggest frown of all, but his wife offered a little wiggly-fingered hello. Lydia was conspicuously absent from the bright-eyed group. She doesn't attend any denomination of church services, likely due to her being a demon from hell.

Once clear of town, I stomped on the gas pedal and reached for the package of dwindling cigarettes, which meant that for the first time in almost two years I'd have to buy more butts to feed the renewed craving. The cell phone on the passenger seat began buzzing. Upon snatching it up and seeing the number calling, I could not remember ever being happier to hear from my wife.

"Hey," I answered and pulled the truck to a stop along the side of a steep gully, "where are you?"

"Is Cliff OK?" Tammy blurted.

"He's fine. I mean, he's…Where are you, for Chrissake?"

"I'm almost home."

"You're not…Are you in the car?" I was ready to explode with recrimination. There's a ton of it stored up in me right now, and it really needs a place to go. "Fuck, Tammy, I told you to get rid of it."

"I did!" she hollered and then hissed, "Asshole! I'm walking home. Why don't you come and get me?"

"I can't. I have to…" Something clicked inside my head. Even in exhaustion, I catch on to something rotten pretty quickly. "What do you mean you're walking?"

"I got rid of the car, like you said. What am I supposed to do, fly home?"

It seemed like a dark watershed moment, one wherein I could stop hoping that things could be resolved and instead give in to the shitstorm gathering fast on the horizon.

"OK, so…" I said gently but gripped the steering wheel as if it were the only thing holding me together, "where's the car?"

"In the woods."

"What woods?" I asked sweetly in a way that would soon be impossible to replicate.

"Well, I was going to drive up to my mom's, but then I decided fuck no, I'm not getting her involved, and where would I get rid of it up there anyway, so I decided to come back."

"OK, I'm ready, Tammy. Where did you leave the fucking car?"

"Up behind the country club."

She could have said the center of town and it would have been only slightly worse news.

"You parked it at *Pure Gold*? What the fuck, Tammy?!"

"I didn't park it at *Pure Gold*! I was trying to get up to the gorg."

The inferno of anger about to ignite in a series of curses got a big bucket of water thrown on it. Her hasty plan, which at first sounded insane, was actually a good idea. The gorge attached to the peak of Tanner Mountain is by far the highest elevation in these parts and fourth highest in the county. Near to the top, it juts off into a near-vertical wall of granite that drops from the cliff face almost four hundred feet in a way that boggles the mind at the power and force which with the old glaciers cut their way through the continent. The river at the base is plenty deep. It would make a fine place to deposit a car that needs disappearing. Only Tammy obviously fell short of her destination.

"How far did you get?"

"About a quarter mile past the club," She fell into the meek and humble tone she adopts after fucking things up. "I thought I turned onto a road and then it was a path and then I got stuck."

"Jesus Christ. Half the town's gonna be up there today!"

"Why?"

"It's Lydia's fucking festival. We gotta—"

"Oh! The Maple Syrup Festival. We gave money to that."

"Where is the damn car exactly?" My words were now coming out harsh and I didn't care.

"Stop yelling at me! I told you. I took the road up past the club and then, about a quarter mile or a little more, there was this, I don't know, like a road…

"It's a logging road. I know where you mean. But it splits, you went down instead of up the mountain. Ah, for fuck's sake."

"I've been walking in the woods for over an hour," Tammy blurted, "so fuck you, Blake!"

"Right. Fuck me," I said easily. "It always seems to end up there."

"I tried my best! Maybe I could've gotten further if you bought me a Jeep like I asked!"

"Bought you a…OK, just listen. Get home and stay with Cliff." I wasn't about to have a blowout with Tammy as the sand was slipping down the hourglass. "I'll take care of the car."

"Get it into the gorge. Somebody said the water's so high cause of all the snow we had. It will disappear, Blake."

"Lucky car," I replied. "You sure you can make it home?"

"You should've asked me that when I was on the mountain."

"Right," I laughed. Even in this dark cave of events, Tammy could always make me chuckle. "I'll take care of it. But you gotta get to Cliff. Let him know it will work out somehow."

"Will it?"

"Fuck if I know. Gotta go. Bye."

At least the kid will be OK for a little while, but for fuck's sake did she have to leave the car so close to the club? It's not that old rides don't get abandoned in the woods—clowns have been dumping an occasional junker out there way before my time— but if some idiot wanders off from the festival drunk on maple syrup whiskey and discovers it, then who knows?

Now, I had a big decision to make. Which to get rid of first, the dead body or the deadly car? Judging that Keith was lying in a fresh grave, killed by two slugs from a gun with my fingerprints all over it, while the car is for the time being out of sight, the dead body won. For the third time in two days, I reluctantly drove out to the old paper mill.

The ride was just long enough for me to get my calendar of events in order. First off, dig up Keith, which was unpleasant but also annoying since I'd only put him in the ground a few hours ago. Next, get the car up to the gorge and drive it over the side without falling in myself. The temptation was strong to dump Keith's body in the trunk of Tammy's car and kill two birds with one stone, but I didn't want to give that motherfucker a ride anywhere, alive or dead.

The river running past his place would do. I'd grab a cinder block from the many he's got propping the porch up and get it bungeed tight to the body and dump it over on of cut-banks where the water's plenty deep to submerge it out of sight. With the recent weather we've been getting, the corpse will hopefully stay that way for a while, probably years. By then, the catfish would've have taken care of that bastard in a way that he rightly deserves.

Even though a dead man was the only person at home, I drove slowly up onto Keith's property. Once there, I parked in front of the house and hustled out back where it had all gone down, while a creepy realization struck me that I was a killer returning to the scene of the crime. It's a scenario played for dramatic effect in movies but from what I've learned, a real-life bad guy usually just kills and gets the hell out of town. That is, except for me, the one bad guy who sticks to the script and suffers the damage, which is why it took such a long time to leave the campfire after shooting dead the gas-station robber in the woods. For hours, I wrestled with the new and horrible realization that there really wasn't any law in the world, just simple choices of doing what's right and wrong.

The grip of confusion and fear was not so strong now. Maybe age numbs the senses to the sting of morality, but the desperation felt the same, and I had to find a way out of a real dark place and get back into the world again. Hopefully, after Keith traded his grave of cold dirt for even colder water, the guilt would ease up.

But when I got around to the back of the house, things didn't seem right. Something had drastically changed.

The red pickup was gone.

I knew exactly where I parked it and after scanning the area to see if it had rolled off somewhere, the reality sunk in that it had been moved. Halting in my tracks and listening for any hint of man-made sound, nothing came back but the natural noise of the woods, a light breeze and the far away roll of the river. Proceeding forward with caution, I discovered that, at some point between the events of this morning and now, someone had indeed taken off with the truck. They had also dug up the grave.

What's worse, the body of the perpetually troublesome and recently expired Keith Griffin was gone.

Chapter Six

Like a whole mess of other angst-ridden people, a good horror story gets me charged up and often delivers a lingering afterglow relief of escaping the vampire or zombie myself. However, outside of scary movies or occasional old episodes of *The Twilight Zone* on television, I do not have the patience for supernatural occurrences in life, despite the ghoulish backstory of my youth in Rock Hollow.

There was the living dead presence of an alcoholic mother who laid down deep trenches of tension around our home that I fell into regularly, ducking for cover and waiting for the gin-fueled storms to pass. There was the monster father who was not happy unless he used his fists to beat another human being at least once a week, and in his rage, he did not cut discounts to women or children.

We were not alone with the constant threat of violence lingering in our unlucky home. The whole town was wracked with poverty and gloom in the long, hungry period following the paper mill closure. Our family happened to cling onto the higher end of the local lower class. My mother was collecting disability from an accident that had occurred a year before the mill shut down, and the state admirably stood by the payments for years, although I'm pretty sure her back healed up fine after about six weeks. My dad drove a plow for the town in the winter and patched potholes in the summer, perhaps lending to the hot and cold temperature of his disposition.

Dark clouds constantly hover around the neighborhoods with families that struggle to put food on the table and properly clothe their bodies, a foul current of human desperation which powers much of the nasty behavior that only begets more hardship and furthers the downward spiral. Growing up around Rock Hollow in the years before the wealthy rediscovered backwoods towns as "cute" retreats from city life required a thick filter of youthful optimism. Without it, nobody could survive explosive scenes of violence at home, skirt past barroom blow-outs that spill out onto the sidewalk in more frequency as the night progresses, and simply ignore the lurid tales of shadowy fiends who lurk the streets and alleyways looking for drink, drugs, or worse, the horrible big-city problems that just don't happen in your hometown, as the saying goes, until they do.

When it became time to take my active part in the big horror show that is life, I gave no quarter to the supernatural because in the line of law enforcement work thrust upon me, there is an explanation for absolutely everything. Even if you crawl through a theory inch by inch and still can't figure things out, then fuck you. There has to be an explanation. Or at least an explanation of why you can't find an explanation because law and order demands a detailed end to the case with a *that's all folks* that the public can chew and swallow while they walk away feeling justified and safe. Therefore, until the day that I'm busting werewolves hunting deer without a license or breaking up a noisy 3 AM rave at Count Dracula's castle, I keep horror stories on the TV and out of my mind.

So then, as I stood staring into that hole, the dirt freshly dug up and its previous occupant long gone, it didn't for a moment seem like I was in the middle of a *Twilight Zone* episode, where the decaying body of Keith Griffin will haunt me to the end of my days. That's binge-watching miniseries material but there's no reason to it. Still, a new kind of sickening panic instantly flushed through me. On any other day, I could've checked the box and moved on, but too much weight was pressing hard on my nerves and I had to locate an answer to this unanswerable occurrence to get back to somewhere normal.

It's only at bizarre times like this that I recall in detail things that I learned in school. Not the dimwit years of the local high school but those two years of college. Maybe because those are shaping up to have been the best years of my life. Sad but true. So, as my physical being stared at that hole for a long, long time, my mind was preoccupied with philosophy.

I started college with a declared major in criminal justice and some kind of vague plan to be a cop or lawyer in Portland or Boston, likely byproducts of my being hooked on *Law & Order* as a kid. Then, during my third semester of a schedule chock-full of criminal and civil justice classes, I had to satisfy a humanities requirement by taking a course in philosophy. The professor was a short, burly, yet gracefully aging gentleman, who coasted across the great philosophical works from the Greeks to modern day with expert yet simple insight and humor in a way that absolutely blew my mind. You didn't talk to folks in my hometown about epistemology or metaphysics or what Plato thought was "the good life". Most people think they are living the good life, and if you question it, they call you crazy and tell you to shut the fuck up. But during that one semester, it felt like the good life for me was sitting back and thinking about the world in a bunch of different ways. Granted, some stuff I just didn't understand. For example, Kant and Sartre were exhausting and often made me fall asleep while trying to do the required reading, but Camus? I got that dude.

What I understood of my friend Albert's view of life, returns to me during chilling moments, such as discovering a body that I buried myself has been dug up and gone missing. It allows me to handle and move on from uncanny and fearful situations. Camus insists that none of us can outrun death, and that fact alone makes for a depressing existence, unless we look at life as one big messed up mistake. We shouldn't be here in the first place. A mound of rock circling a blazing star sounds like the makings for instant disaster. Not to mention that the monkeys would've done a far better job with this planet than human beings determined to fuck up everything we touch. No one should be surprised if things don't make sense. *Nothing* makes any sense, so to try to rationalize oddities is a futile endeavor, akin to spinning wheels in the cosmic muck of everything.

Sadly, as much the professor's class enthralled me during a semester that went by at light speed, the poisonous need to make money pulled me away from philosophy and every other university course. Yet I never lost what Camus gave me: the good sense to doubt macabre, inexplicable matters with a healthy voice of absurd irrationality.

"This is some fucked…up…shit." I whispered, stepping right up to the edge of the hole.

On further inspection, it looked to have been dug up at least several hours before. The soil of the various mounds surrounding it had ice crystals forming at their tops. Likely, somebody loaded the corpse into the truck and was long gone. But who? And to where? Certainly, a frustrating new twist to this endless maze of events, but there really wasn't anything to be done but to get the hell back to town. So, what if someone had stolen the corpse you just killed and buried, also absconding with the rifle that's got my prints on it? There were other dire matters to attend to before I even began to unravel this crazy bullshit.

It did, however, give me second thoughts about getting the judge to approve the warrant. Because, if Keith's dead body suddenly appears in the center of town while the state police are hunting him down, it would put the dogs on my trail way before I could get Cliff and Tammy out of hot water.

To try to block out the whole Keith affair temporarily during the ride back to town, I focused instead on concocting a plan to get the Hinckle brothers to stand down, maybe suggesting that they owed their sister some family mourning time. Even if they hung out with Mariel for an hour or two, it would give me a huge window to steal up to the mountain and get that car dumped into the gorge, then get back to keep an eye on the troublemakers.

Who's kidding who? Those boys probably took turns driving so they could clean their guns and be ready to shoot at the first person who even looked guilty. Maybe I could've warned them that the state police were on their way, but knowing their history around these parts and big brother Ben's present-day mafia wannabe acquaintances, these boys had been in so many spats with the law for so long that it was like sport to them. Also, once you mention that the state police are a higher authority than you, the bad guys tend to stop listening. So, whenever the crazy brothers arrived, I'd have to present just the right appeal to convince them all to back off and let me do my job, which is why I was glad that I packed extra shells for the rifle. The never-ending quandary of defending against maniacs. It requires a lot of firepower.

The relative peace of Main Street was a surprising pleasure as I pulled into town. Easing my hunched shoulders downward and enjoying a normal steady bit of breathing, I cleared my mind of everything for a blissful moment, also forgetting to slow down the truck at the first cross section and nearly adding another checkmark to my book of casualties. Minny Perkin's rattish Pomeranian leaped wildly backwards from its unleashed loitering in the gutter, filling the air with a litany of high-pitched dog profanity. It's yelps only faded after several more blocks, when I got my ride tucked away at the furthest end of town, far away from the dogs and people and, most importantly, the station house, to give the impression that I'm out somewhere doing my job.

Before I could get to Tammy's car, I had to slip into the station to grab Keith's warrant from my desk and then get Barbara to run out for fresh coffee on my dime so I could wipe it off the hard drive. If only Keith Griffin's runaway dead carcass could be wiped away so easily.

There was a small group of people outside of the bakery, so I kept to my dark-alley practices and circled the block, planning to use the back door to the station, take care of business, and be in my truck on the way to the gorge in ten minutes. The only snag in the progress of my hasty plan came when I cut back toward Main Street and the roundabout route took me past the side windows of *Deuces Wild.* Briefly, I glimpsed a couple of patrons conducting their own mid-morning services at the bar, which usually makes me shake my head in humorous disdain. This time it struck me like a siren's call, filling my senses with just enough of a sweet and dangerous song that it wooed me into its trappings.

Inside *The Deuce*, it felt like an instant reprieve. The lighting appeared even dimmer than usual with only a couple of lamps turned on behind the bar, leaving the rest of the place in a gentle shade like the interior of a cave. Mickey takes Sundays off and the fill-in bartender, Jim Lipton, is a music aficionado, so easy jazz was piping through the sound system, maybe Miles Davis, which was a welcome change from the classic rock or country tunes the usual crowd likes to hear over and over.

Of course, the steadfast Elmore was at the bar reading a newspaper and sipping the first poison of the day, or maybe the second. The entire scene was a fractured Norman Rockwell vision of a plain old ordinary America: quiet, sad, and warm with the enchanting presence of liquor holding back all the crazy shit of life for a short while.

What the hell, the day that's coming to me deserved at least a half-dozen drinks. What's one little one? I had a couple of minutes to spare and a cup of coffee could never do the job like a stiff shot of whiskey. That's a proven fact.

"What do you say, El?"

A cruel jest we play on Elmore is to call to him from behind as he is too fat and often too lazy to turn around. Instead, he does this sort of jerking squirm in his seat, a move that he himself nicknamed "the Ankylosaurus" after a dinosaur who he explained had a hard time turning itself about, but could, like Elmore retrieving a fresh drink, execute quick side-to-side motions. So, when I called out, Elmore set about doing the Anky.

"Is that you, Marshall?" he queried, bringing his face back within the limited range his stubby neck allowed until I reached the bar. "Why we haven't seen the likes of you in here this early since you sewed up your gills."

"Yeh, well it was either duck in here or grab coffee at Sam's, and I'm not in the mood for conversation." I pulled a stool out, sat and leaned an elbow on the bar. "Present company excluded."

"Appreciated but not necessary. I've been excluded in various degrees for most of my life."

We laughed and he took a swig of what looked to be a triple bourbon on ice, which got me itching for a sip of something myself. Elmore noticed my searching glance about the place.

"Our mixologist stepped out to retrieve the two of us an egg sandwich and a bagel with ample cream cheese. I do apologize that you missed the run for provisions. I can offer you half of my breakfast. Might I say…" Elmore grinned and pushed his hands against the bottom of the seat, then got up and shuffled around to the back of the bar, "…that you look quite thirsty. James and I have an arrangement. Any drink I pour whilst he's away gets a little check mark on the pad by the register. For you, I shall substitute a little star. What'll it be?"

"Gotta be a quick one Just a little whiskey," I barely made it sound like booze wasn't why I was here, "Two fingers."

"A gentleman pours nothing less than three," Elmore admonished, and a stiff drink appeared before me in seconds.

"Now," he went on after waddling back to his perch and lifting his drink, "what shall we memorialize?"

"Here's to drinking when you ain't supposed to."

It certainly felt like the wrong thing to do, but I was so out of sorts that I couldn't imagine anything more appealing than that highball glass full of ice chunks and rye whiskey. The draining events of the last twelve hours and the mess of trouble ahead managed to strip all the taboos away from the brown booze in my glass, the evil cure-all that I'd fought hard to avoid for well over a year. Those first days had been hell, sleeping like shit, sometimes sweating and shaking. Once over the fence, the only thing left behind inside me was a deep and longing desire for a belt of mash or ten. Not to mention the weekly Alcoholics Anonymous meetings that I used to frequent over in Oakfield; hours and hours of reminders about what shits we all are when we're drunk.

Without fail, I'd leave the basement of the town rec center with a screaming headache from the thick fog of cigarette smoke, and coffee the texture of melted fudge. Around nineteen months passed since my last drink, so I chose to look at this like a special occasion, which in many ways it was. For all the wrong reasons.

"Lovely." Elmore clinked his glass to mine and took a hefty sip. "If you don't mind me saying, Marshall, you look a bit drawn."

"Haven't slept much." The taste of the whiskey on my tongue took my breath away at first. "Trouble at home. Trouble at work. Trouble all over."

"Employment hazards I can fully relate to," Elmore drawled. "Domestic issues not so much. Unease with the missus, I assume?"

"Always." The second larger sip brought back the power of booze mixed with the comfort of conversation, further enhanced by the sounds of ice tinkling in a tipped back glass, and sweet jazz on the player. Damn, I'm in trouble. "But that's nothing. The wife's always on my back. This time I got big problems with my kid too and…Ah hell."

Elmore seemed to be mocking my tiny sips with his own huge gulps, but when he spoke his tone was sympathetic rather than patronizing.

"Oh, I can speak volumes about teenagers." He leaned back in his chair and tapped the newspaper in front of him. "You could fill a daily rag with my travails of wrestling knowledge into and out of young, scattered minds. Truly, just this week I battered my head against my laptop trying to move an online class of fifteen through Miller's *Death of a Salesman*. College freshmen, mind you, who are paying to be enlightened, or at least their parents are, and they can't find space in their limpid brains for something written in 1948. How are we expected to pass the baton of classical Greek tragedy when you can't awaken torpid cranial pathways with 20th-century English?"

"I read that one in high school, thought it was just OK," I replied, clasping my half-empty glass with the grip of one who expects a second round soon.

"Then your teacher was a Neanderthal."

"I liked A Streetcar Named Desire better."

"Because that was a play about Neanderthals. And Tennessee Williams was sexy. Arthur Miller is not sexy. Imagine the narcotics that Marilyn Monroe was bursting with when she married him? But I tell you, we've crossed an abyss with the young folks. It used to be that students would go light up a few joints and plow their way through the old great books so that they could fuck off with Vonnegut or Kerouac or even Updike, the filthy son-of-a-bitch. Now, the next great generation measures how deep their personal libraries are by how many fucking Harry Potter books they've made it through."

"I like when you get surly." I grinned and cocked my head. "I've got to catch you this early in the day more often."

"What brings you in here, Marshall?"

"Huh?"

"Well, you know, we all love your visits while you're sniffing out assorted acts of injustice, but…" Elmore said, cocking his head toward me and meeting my curious expression with a warm, knowing smile, "...you're simply not one of us anymore."

"One of what?" I chuckled, but he was more right than he knew.

"The lost souls of Rock Hollow. The wastrels. The wanton. You've climbed out of this cave and found the light."

"And what did it get me?"

"Oh, come now. Weighing the existence of a drunkard against that of a family man, only one amounts to a proper life."

"I may drink sodas and fruit juices these days, present company excluded," I lifted the glass and winked at it in acknowledgement. "But I sure as hell ain't living a good life, and sobriety only makes it worse. It used to be really nice drinking my problems away."

"Is it the death of that boy that has you so rattled?"

By now, I was too tired to be startled by the question and Elmore was the last person to root out gossip so I went honest with him.

"Yeh."

"Because you've not apprehended the suspect?" Elmore finished his drink with an elegant pinky in the air.

"Yup, that's definitely part of it."

"Meanwhile, when you do arrest someone, which I'm quite sure you will, the only thing to change is that justice shall be served. The dead will remain dead, so there's no rush to repair that."

"Can't have kids getting run down like it's…"

"Neither can we have white-collar criminals in our midst, or insurance fraudsters, or tax evaders, or sexual deviants, or kleptomaniacs, or gamblers, or arsonists, or…Well I can stop there. I probably covered most of the population with sexual deviants. What I'm saying is you could solve a thousand crimes and it would do nothing to change the character of the people of this town. So, cut yourself a break, Marshall. You're one of our betters, in my opinion."

"Do you…" The question lingered in my mind for a couple of moments before I let it go. "In your learned experience, do you think some folks are just born bad?"

"I think we're all born God-awful. Any spark of good that appears is a fucking miracle."

"Like the…suspect in this case? They killed someone, but…if they get away, they might go on and live out a half-way decent life, right?"

"Presumably, if they keep away from starchy foods and television."

"Do you think anything like a curse follows somebody like that?"

"Karmic vengeance? Most assuredly. If not at the hands of others, then certainly in the tortuous recesses of the mind. Now we're veering into Dostoevsky's territory which means I must switch to vodka."

Elmore slid from his stool but didn't take two steps when he turned around and looked at me with trusting eyes.

"I will say that even when karma wreaks havoc against presidents, kings, or even the lowly Raskolnikov, every last one of them has the ability to forgive themselves. That, I believe, is the only divine spark we've got. And with that, fuck all. I need a drink!"

Before Elmore could get half-way around the bar, the door opened and Jim stepped inside. The concerned look on his face made me suddenly remember that I'd left my cell phone in the truck.

"Sheriff! Geez!" Jim rushed over to us. "I'm glad you're here; there's trouble at the bakery."

"Were they out of cream-cheese, again?" El squawked as he retook his seat.

"I was waiting for my order, having a smoke outside," Jim rattled, unable to get the words out fast enough, "when this big red pickup pulls right onto the sidewalk and these guys—"

"Three of them?" I interrupted, standing quickly and moving to go.

"Yup. Real goons. Busted right into the bakery, and now they won't let nobody out."

Jim was deeply concerned but not enough to volunteer to help. Instead, he went around the bar.

"Well, that's my cue." I tipped the glass for a few pieces of whisky-flavored ice to crunch on and headed out. "Elmore, a pleasure."

"Why don't you stay here for now?" he suggested gently.

"These guys were geared up like soldiers," Jim said, pacing behind the bar, "and that pickup had a stocked gun rack. Stocked!"

"Not many around here that don't," I joked, but any humor was long gone.

"Keep the peace, Marshall," Elmore instructed, "If you can't, then do try to keep yourself alive."

"See you, fellas."

Jim stopped me before I could step outside. "You want me to help, Sheriff? I mean, I'm a little spooked but…I'll help you."

"No thanks, bud." I turned and acknowledged the goodwill with a two-fingered salute. "You just keep one of those bar stools warm for me. After this, I'm gonna need a happy hour or two."

Bolstered by Jim's modest act of courage, a small gesture that had changed my perspective of the man entirely, I focused on the last notes of jazz escaping the tavern before I closed the door behind me— a long, fragile horn solo which seemed more beautiful than any I'd heard before. If that was Miles Davis playing, then the tracks that he laid down deserved to live forever.

I walked, not too fast or too slow, toward the bakery. The crowd outside had dispersed and, just like Jim had said, a big red Ford pickup was parked across the sidewalk, empty and idling away loudly, kicking out clouds of exhaust smoke like a true transport from hell.

Catching a glance through the storefront window, it looked like the bakery had a fair number of customers standing around, but not a single one was sipping coffee or eating treats. Too many nervous faces and downcast gazes on display for a joint that sold cupcakes. A big body was blocking the door from the inside, and only after my rapping loudly on the glass did the large frame turn to me. The youngest of the clan, Derrick Hinckle, scowled and scratched at his frizzy bush of beard, making his face look much larger and more stupid. His empty brown eyes, just visible under an orange ski cap, blazed to life when he caught a good look at me.

"Get outta the way!" I demanded and rapped a loud couple of knocks on the glass so close to his face that he flinched.

He turned back to say a few words to someone while I glanced in at the stressed and concerned faces of the folks crowding along the walls and counter space. Only after getting a response did Derrick move aside and allow me to push open the door. Although the big fella barely gave me room to enter.

"Get this truck off the sidewalk right the hell now!" I bellowed.

The only face-to-face meetings about the illegal dump site had been our kicking Ben's lackey's asses. He and I had sworn each other up and down but entirely on the phone, so I hadn't seen any of the Hinckle brothers in person for close to ten years, but you could pick them out of a crowd any day of the week. Each was fully dressed in the martial fashion that some modern hunters have adopted, with black camo suits, full zip up jackboots, and various assortments of gear buckled, strapped, or fastened with Velcro to their bodies, including a knife on Derrick's belt that appeared large enough to saw down small trees.

"Everybody all right?" I asked while looking around, getting only silence in return from the spooked patrons and staff, a thick tension mixing strangely with the odor of coffee and fresh pastry.

"We're doin' just fine," Ben Hinckle replied from the back of the store, as wiry and menacing as memory served, maybe more. "Just askin' some questions is all."

Ben was the eldest of the brothers, a thin, muscular man of medium height who had lost all his hair early and tended to meet the world with a perpetual squint. He had been many years ahead of me in school and a great football player but had misspent his down time outside of practice and games breaking into and entering people's homes and businesses, sometimes for loot, other times just for the hell of it.

"OK, everybody out," I ordered and tried to pull the door open wider.

Derrick slid his boot in the way. His voice was low and raspy. "We ain't done."

"Is this how the day's gonna start?" I turned from Derrick and stared Ben Hinckle down for a long, silent moment.

"OK, everybody, go on back home and stuff your faces with doughnuts," Ben finally responded. "Thank you all for bein' no fuckin' use at all."

When I flung the door open, the bell attached gave a violent tinkle, and the scared folks filed out fast. Most were silent. Only when an older man voiced a "thank-you Sheriff" on the way past us did Derrick get mischievous, stopping the old guy with an abrupt hand to the chest, then leaning over and peering into the bag that the man had cradled in his arm.

"Anythin' in there for me?"

The man's startled eyes searched mine for the correct response.

"Nope. City ordinance. We don't allow folks to feed the wild animals," I said cooly, "so go ahead on your way, sir."

"Who you callin' an animal?" the middle brother, Dicky, shouted from his spot near the cash register.

I hadn't noticed Dicky at first, and that's dangerous. Although a close race with his other siblings, Dicky was clearly the meanest of the three. He had been in the army for a stretch until a mismatched barroom brawl with some marines left him with his face rearranged and a dishonorable discharge. Apparently near the end, Dicky was lashing out at his enemies with a broken beer bottle. Because a couple of marines ended up in the emergency room, he took the discharge over four years in the stockade. He was no taller than Ben and similarly bald but his hair was gone by choice with a buzzcut right to the scalp, ripped with muscles like a doped-up Russian weightlifter, and a scowling face that was born to be in mug shots, tense and angry with a nose that looks freshly broken. Dicky lived life too highly strung and just plain itchy, sweeping the vote for the brother most likely to go ballistic.

A young girl had stuck her head through the red curtain that separates the bakery's kitchen from the storefront. "Can we go too?"

"Hell, no!" Derrick barked. "Get the hell back there and cook me some breakfast! Two eggs over easy with a side of your buns!"

He and Dicky shared a round of goon's laughter.

"Get your things and go," I said as soon as the brother's outburst had died down. "You and whoever else is back there."

"You're awful bossy," Ben remarked, taking a sip of coffee from a paperboard cup.

The girl came out of the kitchen along with a young man. They both kept their eyes on the ground as they hustled toward the door.

"Hold on," I said. "Did these fellas pay for their coffee?"

They both stopped, and the girl kept her head down, but the boy shot a nervous look my way.

"Pay em," I demanded, and Derrick snickered, so I raised my voice. "I know the lady who owns this place, and she's good people. So are these kids. Pay em."

"Pay em, Dicky," Ben said and slurped the rest of his coffee, tossing the empty cup at but not into a nearby trash bin.

"Why me? I didn't have nothin'," Dicky whisper-whined at his brother.

"Cause I said," Ben spoke slowly, and Dicky responded by digging into his pocket and shelling some bills onto the counter.

"Collect it later." I waved the two out the door. "Go wait at the diner. You can come back and close up when I tell you."

They scurried away as if they never planned on coming back ever again.

When I shut the door and turned to the brothers, Ben was the first to speak while he slid some chairs around a table.

"Have a seat, Sheriff," he offered, "We got some catchin' up to do."

The other two moved to the chairs but my spot by the door was just fine.

"I'm good."

"Not good enough to catch the fucker that killed our nephew," Dicky spat, kicking a chair out and depositing himself on it.

"Fellas, I'll say it once and I mean it. I am truly sorry for your family's loss." I spoke evenly, taking a step closer to them. As Ben was the only one still standing, I rested my gaze on him. "I know your sister pretty well. I've been working all weekend on it and the Staties are due here any time."

"Staties ain't for shit," Derrick blurted, apparently just to add color to the chat.

"Don't think I forgot about you hasslin' money and manpower outta me over that property…but we didn't come up for a fight with you." Ben smiled but there was a smolder to it. "Shit, we coulda done that any time. So, during this friendly visit to crappy, old Rock Hollow, you can sort of think of us as helpers."

"You can help by leaving everybody the hell alone and letting the law do its work."

"Hear that boys?" Ben rapped his knuckles on the table. "We're to leave folks alone. That'll be easy cause we ain't lookin' for people. What we're huntin' down is a vehicle."

"A sedan," Derrick added, "a dark one."

"What sedan?" I forced myself to breathe easily and keep a cool expression. They already knew the color and make. These goons were ten steps ahead of where I thought they'd be.

"You don't even know what the hell you're lookin' for, Sheriff. For fuck's sake, you need us! We got friends in high places," Ben went on. "Dicky served with a dude who works for the Bureau. We told him 'bout Philly and he talked to a buddy at the Safety Board. Seems that a truck or Jeep would've knocked the kid down. Only a regular car would've knocked him in the air."

"I've looked all over town. There's been nothing—"

"We also got some paint chips. Tiny ones. My sister didn't have it in her to identify the body, so we had to go to that sad excuse of a morgue you got. Fuckin' faggot undertaker's got the kid layin' on ice like a fuckin' popsicle! Anyway, said he got some pieces of paint from Philly's arm."

Five more steps forward for the brothers and ten back for me. I hadn't wanted to involve Dan Miller any more than he already was and had even ignored a couple of texts he'd sent overnight. Hell, when it's all said and done, he may become a witness for the prosecution against my whole family, so I figured the less I said to him the better. Still, who on earth would've guessed that the Hinckle brothers had enough brains to conduct a forensics investigation?

"Listen to me." Although truly alarmed, my demeanor didn't crack a bit. "This is interfering with a legal matter. There's nothing—"

"We ain't here for nothin'. We came to find the fucker that ran down Philly!" Dicky slammed his fist on the table and stood up.

"Fuck this. Tell em what we need and let's go."

Ben shot a wildly angry look at Dicky and then turned back to me and resumed his impersonation of a sane man.

"We need you to get us a list of registered cars in town," he suggested firmly. "Dicky's buddy said he'd take a look and pick out our prime suspects."

"I'm gonna eat this." Derrick had fallen out of the conversation and was reaching for a doughnut that sat untouched on a small plate at a table nearby. "It just got left behind."

He took a big chomp that left sugar powder on his beard, and I let the slight indiscretion go as a tiny lost battle in the wider war. Dicky paced around the place while Ben sat back and folded his arms, waiting patiently for my reply. A search for cars without the registration records would take days, but with a list of addresses they'd be able to check on most everybody by the end of the afternoon. This gang needed to be held back, at least until the state police arrived, and I didn't expect to see a cruiser pulling up outside any time soon.

"Records like that don't go out to the public," I replied, "no matter who asks."

"We're not askin'." Dicky stepped up to me, a strong odor of liquor on his breath, clarifying that the biggest nut in the family was also a drunk.

"Let me tell you…I've been in situations like this before. Where a lawman knows that he should be helpin' a family that got wronged but just can't wiggle out from behind his badge." Ben stood up and strolled to the counter and picked up the bills that Dicky had left. "Well, Sheriff, our story is that we came in here peacefully and was just havin' a talk with some locals when you bust in the place. First you kick all the witnesses out, which is appreciated, then you accuse my brother of stealin' a doughnut. We say it ain't so, and you draw your gun on us."

Ben lifted an arm and leaned it on the counter, then pulled his jacket back to show off the gun on his hip—a jet-black Desert Eagle

"Then what happens?" I spoke to Ben, but Dicky had my attention as he drew closer with little steps.

"Let's just say you don't need to hear no more of that story," Ben answered as if speaking to a child, "seein' you wouldn't be in it for long. We're not fuckin' around, so get us the list and then get out of the way."

"This one ain't been touched, neither." Derrick was now perusing the other tables for abandoned sweets, tearing a huge chomp from a cinnamon bun. "Ohhh thass goob."

"Any of you guys on probation?" I thought a change of perspective was necessary. "Or you're just all-out looking for new reasons to go to prison?"

"Who the fuck you think you're talkin' to?" Ben roared in his first real flash of anger. "I coulda sent an army up here to take care of this. But we got a sister with her heart broke. You might be an alright dude, don't think so but also don't fuckin' care. You're a hick town badge that's gonna either help us or get hurt bad. Now which is it?"

I had expected big trouble from these men, but it hadn't occurred to me that I'd wind up in a doughnut shop shootout. Derrick would be no trouble—he was busy with an egg sandwich in his face from his third table raid—but the other two had a way about them that showed a lust for any shade of violence.

"I don't know shit about computers. You're outta luck." I confessed, somewhat truthfully, and confident that this trio hadn't a tech whiz amongst them.

"That's OK. We'll show you how to turn it on," Ben replied and started walking for the door. "Derrick, stop stuffin' your face! We're goin' to the station."

"What about him?" Dicky jerked a thumb at me.

Ben fixed a harsh, mocking gaze on me. "Sheriff don't know shit about computers, so he can just fuck off here and have some breakfast."

The others followed Ben when he moved out of the bakery, and there seemed to be no good way to stop them because two things needed to happen at once. Barbara had to get the hell out of the station house and go home. Also, the office hard drive had to disappear. Both needed to go down in the minute or so it would take the brothers to walk over there. Im-fucking-possible. But hell, today the impossible needed to give a little bit for law and order to prevail. Unfortunately, wicked fate was holding steadfast as ever when a slap to each of my pants pockets reminded me that my cell phone was in the truck.

"Hold on, damn it." I let it come out plenty surly and it seemed to get their attention as they halted on the sidewalk. "No one's scaring my help out of a job. I need all I can get. I'll take you over."

Derrick and Dicky looked at me with surprise, but Ben was nothing but suspicious, and who cares? For the moment, we all stood in front of their idling gas-guzzler of a truck. As fast as the crowd had jettisoned the bakery, a surprising number of them were still lingering on the nearest corners to watch the rest of the action play out.

"But first," I continued, "you got to know that when folks around here found out about your nephew Philly's accident, they…suffered a shock the same as your family. Not anywhere near as personal, but…that kind of news digs deep into people, and we're a small town, so we feel things like that pretty big when they come along."

Perhaps the brothers knew I was stalling for time so that something, anything really, would come to mind to get Barbara and the hard drive safely away, but for the moment they were genuinely caught up in my pop-up sidewalk sermon and none of them took another step. Figuring that doling out cigarettes to the group from the dwindling pack would buy another few moments, I withdrew it from my jacket, and just as Ben was about to say something, I kept on preaching.

"I mean, it is Sunday. The holiest day of the week. You saw that crowd in the bakery, probably about a tenth of our total population was over at church this morning. That's pretty pious for a hick town. I don't know about you fellas, but Sunday morning usually starts with a shot of whatever I was drinking Saturday night, am I right?"

Derrick and Ben were quickly losing patience, but at the mention of liquor, Dicky got dreamy for a second and then fell right back into hate.

"Just shut the hell up and get us them addresses," he growled.

"Right, but I just want to make it clear…"

Before I could stall them with a few words about freedom of information until they completely lost patience, one of those uncanny yet beautiful random events of life blessed me with its timely grace. It arrived smack in the middle of Main Street, rolling silently past the brothers' pickup in her electric moon-lander. Lydia Bernard was likely on her way to harass her help during the set-up of the Maple Syrup Festival and so kindly provided the stroke of fortune which poked its way through my run of bad luck. It was her staring me down with a disgusted grimace, which prompted my inspiration to transform that ugly, old crow into a tremendous load of bullshit.

"Shit, there she is," I gasped. "Son-of-a-bitch, I got to go get that lady."

"Who?" Dicky demanded.

"That gal in the electric truck right there! She's the prime suspect right now. Biggest lush in town. I gotta question her."

"That lady?" Ben asked and kept an eye on Lydia pulling away at her usual thoughtlessly too-fast clip. "You think she done it?"

"Can't tell til I question her, but she sure does drink like a fish and tears around the streets like she owns the place."

"Bitch!" Derrick added.

"Yup, she's that too. So, wait right here until I get a look at—"

"Derrick, come on!" Ben shouted and ran around to the driver's side of the truck. "We'll get her. Dicky, you go with the sheriff and get that list from the station."

He jumped in and leaned on the horn in attempt to hustle Derrick, who was having trouble opening the door with his sticky, glazed hands. Once Derrick fumbled his way inside, Ben kicked the truck into reverse, and his beady, slitted eyes met mine with a look of "don't you dare be fucking with me" before the duo tore away after Lydia.

"OK, come on," I said to Dicky, who began following way too close on my heels.

We headed in the opposite direction of the station, but he knew no better. The idea of taking him into an alley and knocking him cold was attractive but could result in one of us getting shot, which would slow me down, particularly if I took the bullet. Also, he kept a pace behind me that guessed at my every move. What we needed was to build some trust quickly. Fortunately, we passed by the perfect place for it.

"Look at that." I slowed my steps in front of *The Deuces Wild.* "The watering hole's open for business."

When I turned to lay some coaxing words on Dicky, he was already staring through the tavern's window like a kid drooling outside a candy shop.

"Want to grab a quick one?"

"Better not. C'mon." He furrowed his brow, motioning for me to proceed.

"I tied one on hard last night." I chuckled. "Could really use just a double whiskey. We'll kick it back before they even catch up to that lady."

Dicky's annoyance melted away and left him licking his lips. He looked back once to where his brothers had torn down the street and then back at me, pointing a single finger upward.

"Just one, real quick. You're buyin'."

"Of course." Sporting a wide grin, I graciously led the son-of-a-bitch inside.

"So, what happened?" Jim bellowed as soon as we stepped in, while Elmore studied us with deep curiosity upon our reaching the bar.

"It was just a misunderstanding. This is my friend Dicky Hinckle. He just got into town with his brothers." I gave a warning look to Jim, but he was slightly turned away, finishing a call on his cell phone. "Hey, El. Meet Dicky."

"Greetings, sir." Elmore said warmly, but a knowing glance told me that he was wise to the situation.

"Yeh, hey." Dicky brushed off El and hollered to Jim, "Two double whiskeys and hurry it up."

Jim turned to us and winced at the sight of my companion. He ended the call with a shake to his voice but recovered quickly enough and soon placed two shot glasses on the bar top and reached for a bottle.

"No, not that rotgut," I said and held a hand over the glass into which he was about to pour. "This is a guest from out of town. His nephew's the one that got hit by the car. I want my special single-barrel whiskey."

Jim traded a brief glance between me and El as he prepared to go along with the ruse but also proved to be not nearly as good a performer as the old man.

"OK. What do you want me to do?" he asked mechanically and rested a concerned gaze on me.

"Go get it out of the cellar," I replied.

"Out of the…cellar?" Jim repeated the last word slowly.

"That figures," I broke in quickly before he gave us away, adding a round belly laugh. "Mickey didn't tell you where he hides it, did he?"

"Of course, he didn't!" Elmore shouted, almost eager to get into the game. "Why James couldn't keep his Irish paws off the good stuff if you locked it in a safe. I remember the time we got that case of bourbon shipped up for the summer fireworks. By the time the night sky was lit up by flares and sparklers, so too was the inside of Jim's head from a bottle of fine Kentucky hellfire."

Elmore laughed loudly, and I joined in while Jim giggled in confusion.

"So go get it," Dicky said.

"You go on, Sheriff." Elmore waved me toward the back of the place. "Only you know where Mickey stashes things. If your friend is new in town, I must inform him of the secret house on the turnpike where he might spend some quality time with certain ladies of questionable reputation."

"You got a whorehouse round here now?" Dicky's eyes widened.

"Oh, so many of them," Elmore replied. "They pop up like rodent colonies."

Good old Elmore made me want to deputize him on the spot. Instead, I stepped around the bar and gave a confident nod to Jim.

As I was ducking through the door to the back, Dicky barked a loud warning.

"You got about twenty seconds."

"Time will slow down once you get a kick from this bottle. Be right back," I assured him.

As Elmore held Dicky's rapt attention by detailing the fictional, circuitous route to the cathouse on the turnpike, I stepped into the big, dark rectangular supply room behind the bar. The only light came through a single small window, and there were of course no doors leading to a staircase or anywhere else. Everyone but Dicky Hinckle knows that *The Deuces Wild* has no basement and the back exit was sealed up with several large padlocks and chains to keep the lushes of town from pinching a month's supply of booze. The space was cluttered with beer kegs, boxes of liquor and cleaning materials that don't get used often enough, and after maneuvering around many cases of empty beer bottles, I reached the window.

Elmore's loud and lively voice back in the bar covered up the couple of squeaks that the window frame gave from my struggle to get it open, but after rising half-way it stuck fast. I took off my gun belt and dropped it to the ground outside and then stuck my head and hands out, forcing one shoulder through at a time until another big squeeze got my waist onto the windowsill and upper body dangling into the alleyway. However, my butt and legs did not want to follow.

I am not a fat man. Just like any other red-blooded American, most times steaks, pizzas, and submarine sandwiches do not last long in my presence and because of it the inevitable spread of age is plugging up my plans and frittering precious seconds, so I simply thought myself thin, sucked in my gut and pushed against the building. The sill squeezed hard at my thighs, adding yet another float to the pain parade, until the frame gave out with a loud crack, and I tumbled out on the dusty gravel of the back alley.

After hastily gathering my gun belt to the sounds of Dicky inside making a racket, I hurried out of the alley and onto the street behind the bar. There was no time to get to the station without Dicky catching up to me, so I headed for my truck at a full sprint. Turning onto Main Street, I covered the four blocks without even turning to see if the son-of-a-bitch had exited the bar. A few folks had to duck for cover as I barreled past them.

Arriving at the truck, I grabbed the two-way's handset because I wasn't about to deal with lousy cell phone reception.

"Barbara or Stacey or whoever," I said between big gulps of breath, "Pick up now!"

"Hey, Sheriff, I'm here." Barbara's voice crackled back and never sounded so good. "What's the matter? Over."

"Fuck the over and outs, Barbara. Listen to me. The crazy Hinckle brothers are in town. You gotta get outta there right now!"

"What? Why? Shit! OK," she spluttered.

"And listen. You gotta grab the hard drive."

"The what?"

"The computer. Rip it out of the wall if you have to. Just get it outta there now!!"

I didn't wait for an answer. At first, fumbling with the keys, I got the truck going and tore off toward the station, screeching to a halt a few moments later outside of *The Deuce* as Jim came outside holding a hand to his head.

"What happened?" I yelled through the window.

"That guy got pissed when he saw you was gone," Jim replied with a pained face. "Made us tell him where your station's at. Hit me in the head and knocked Elmore off his stool."

"Is El all right?"

Jim nodded, “Yeah. He’s having a drink. What the hell’s—”

There was no time for chit-chat with only five more blocks to the station. When I pulled up, it became clear that Dicky had beaten me there. After turning to watch my truck arrive, he threw me the middle finger, opened the front door, and disappeared inside.

“Ah, hell,” I sighed and slowly stepped out.

Without a doubt, keeping those addresses out of their hands would’ve held things in check for a little while. Now the clock was ticking down to their discovery that our car is a potential match to their target and has also curiously gone missing.

Heading into the station to keep Dicky from wrecking the place, I caught sight of movement in the row of hedges at the corner of the building. It stopped and then started again, this time the foliage shaking furiously until Barbara sort of stepped-fell out and onto the sidewalk, lugging the computer tower in both hands, with a couple of scratches on her face from the bush branches.

“Go on now!”

She shot me a nervous grin and jogged awkwardly to her car. I watched her pull away and tear down the street and, in another second or two, a frustrated Dicky burst out of the station. In almost perfect bad-guy timing, the roar of Ben Hinckle’s pickup approached from behind us.

“What the fuck’s goin on? There ain’t no computer in there!” Dicky howled as the truck pulled up.

Dicky charged right up to me with clenched hands, and I did not hesitate in planting a hard fist across his face. He dropped like a sack of potatoes at my feet, and I stepped over him to welcome the other two, who had jumped out of the truck just in time to see me level their brother.

“Self-defense! Self-defense!” I shouted, arms aloft.

“That lady said you're full of shit!” Ben roared, pointing a finger at me. “Said she had nothin’ to do with it.”

“You let her go?!” I put on a shocked face that could win an Academy Award.

"She said you—" Derrick began.

"She's not only a drunk but the biggest liar in town! Geez, fellas! You had her in the palm of your hands!"

Neither one of them made an immediate move on me, and we all watched Dicky make several attempts to stand while trying to shake off the bells in his head.

"Sorry about that, kid." I bent over to give him a hand. While he was getting to his feet I leaned and whispered, "I won't tell Ben you've been drinking."

The gamble being that Dicky's boozing was a major annoyance to his brother, and having once been a drunk myself, it figured as a safe and familiar bet.

"Badge or not. At some point, I'm gonna fuck you up today," he growled and then turned to Ben. "Computer was gone when I got here."

"Shit," Ben spat, "Why does that not surprise me. All right, Sheriff. Where is it?"

"Shoot, I gave my dispatcher the weekend off. She must have taken her work home."

"Bullshit," Derrick blurted. "Where she live, then?"

I shrugged and widened my eyes. "Not sure. She's kinda new."

"You know that lady you sicked us on said she's gonna fire you." Ben stepped up real close with an acrid mix of body stink and tobacco. For the first time, I saw he had one brown eye and one green. "Well, it's your lucky day. We got a sudden openin' in the manhunt department. Welcome aboard!"

He slapped me hard on the shoulder and headed back to the truck. Derrick stood and smiled a wicked grin, and Dicky looked to be considering shooting me on the spot.

"I've got work to do," I objected.

"Yeh! Findin' the motherfucker that ran down Philly!" Ben spun around and screamed with such force that it took us all by surprise. "That's exactly what we're doin'. And we're invitin' a sheriff's escort to keep things nice and proper. OK? OK?!"

I let them all stand there good and long before responding.

"I'll follow you for a while but—"

"That's right. We're a team!" Ben hollered and banged on the hood of his truck on the way to the driver's side. "Let's go, team!"

Sticky situations in the past have taught me that, when the battle turns against you, and this one wasn't looking too good, it's best to duck your head, let the shit fly and go with the flow. That is, until you get a chance to sneak off and get the hell to safety. At best, that would probably entail knocking another brother or two upside the head, a welcome opportunity when it arrives.

"I said I'd help for a bit," I huffed with resignation and stepped past Dicky.

"A bit? That's all you got for us, fuckface?" Dicky spat on the ground at my feet.

Derrick and Dicky joined Ben in his vehicle and they watched me close while I walked to my truck. While I eased into the driver's seat slowly, waiting for a bright idea to arrive, Ben pulled alongside and leaned out the window like he was ordering junk food at a drive-through, eyeing me suspiciously.

"Help us get this business done, and we'll get outta your hair. Right after we let you and Dicky work things out."

"Probably want to start heading out to the west side of town," I advised. "More houses, more cars."

"Lead the way, Sheriff," Ben cooed with a smirk that begged to be wiped away.

I took them on the long route so that we could eat up as much time as possible. For the moment, Tammy and Cliff were safe and quiet on the east side, and the car was sitting high up on the mountain. Who knew where the wandering corpse named Keith was by now but it didn't matter.

Here we were, a tiny convoy trekking through town and for a second it brought on a bizarre flashback to those long-lost teenager days when my gang would skip school, load into a couple of trucks, and drive out to the lake to tan, swim, and smoke pot. Only this trip didn't seem like it would wind up with a nice, stoned dip in chilly waters, not in the least. It was a dark cloud of violence sweeping through town as we headed toward something that felt a lot closer to drowning.

Chapter Seven

The west side of town comprises over a mile of neighborhoods, a few new developments, but mostly older streets with sparse, simple dwellings branching from Main Street on the way toward the bypass. Residents of these over one-hundred rental homes are a good chunk of the local population. Lots of families have been here forever and occupy the same jobs that have been around for just as long. This is where our mechanics, butchers, bakers, plumbers, and general laborers hang their hats. Many are families that had their livelihoods ripped away when the paper mill closed, a dark period when machinists, operators, and shippers found themselves having to take on any seasonal work such as picking apples or chopping firewood and other quick-cash gigs, to keep the lights on and bellies full.

I consider the West Side to be the heart of the town—good people who can't get away from bad times and it would take one hell of a miracle to get the nut job Hinckle brothers through there without causing any disturbances. Hardscrabble folks like to be left alone on a Sunday.

The initial sign of trouble arose before we'd even reached the first house. Ben yanked his vehicle into park as soon as we turned into the nearest neighborhood, and both Dicky and Derrick got out and walked over to my truck. Ben banged a quick U-turn and pulled up alongside me.

"Gotta see to somethin'," he said with a frown. "Boys will ride with you for now. Be back in a few."

Ben tore away as Dicky opened the passenger door and let Derrick get in the back while he rode shotgun, somewhat literally, because I'm sure he had a firearm on him somewhere. When I slowed down at the driveway of the first residence, a ranch-style home whose obvious roof issues were covered liberally with blue tarps to hold off the rain, Dicky jumped right out before I could come to a full stop.

"Hey, slow down!" I objected loudly and looked back at Derrick, who wasn't making a move to go anywhere. "Sneak up on some of these people and you'll wind up with a gunfight in the front yard."

"Maybe that's what we're lookin' for," Derrick giggled.

Now I understood fully that Ben was the brains, as damaged as it is, of this outfit and Dicky the temper, but young Derrick was just the dumb-as-fuck one.

I managed to call Dicky back over to the truck. After some haggling over the likely results of diplomacy versus brute force, the brothers agreed to let me knock on front doors before they started snooping around yards and garages. My routine was the same at the first dozen stops: apologizing for the intrusion to whoever answered the door and then being real clear that the stooges in my care want only to take one look at the makes and models of the cars and we would be on our way. Still, some folks objected to the mid-morning hour while others flat-out hollered about invasion of privacy. A big guy who lived in a tiny dwelling that looked to be held up by just the paint job took great offense at being bothered and he and Dicky almost came to blows. A few of the homes were families I knew well, and Joe Ferguson's wife handed me over a fresh-baked blueberry muffin. I ate it with overt satisfaction in front of Derrick's famished glare on the way to the next stop, where we were presented with a different kind of welcome.

After knocking at the mildew-spotted front door to no avail and waiting on the front porch while the nitwits snooped behind the house, a man's scream came from the backyard, sounding as if he had been run through with a sword. The deep-throated barking and snarls of a dog followed. Before I could make it around the house, Dicky came sprinting past me with Derrick close behind, holding his left forearm and swearing up a storm. With no monster in immediate pursuit of them, I peeked around the corner to see a big, mean pit bull with the gray and black fur of its neck squeezed tight in a metal collar attached to a fat chain, stretched to its taut limit from a stake in the ground. The animal was just about foaming at the mouth and pulling on that chain like he'd broken out of it before, and neither of the brothers had the good sense to estimate how much of the small backyard the dog could cover under restraint.

The answer was most of it, including the area around two parked cars, a muscle Camaro with bad body rot and a Jeep that I vaguely remembered pulling over once. The instant I turned back to the truck, a hairy, heavyset man wearing only gray sweatpants came vaulting out of the house with an aluminum baseball bat in his hands. Although my preference was to let him use the bat on both brothers Hinckle, I placed myself between him and the others, pulling my jacket open to flash the badge and resting a hand on my sidearm.

"Back off! Sheriff's Department!" I warned him.

"The fuck ya doin' in my yard!"

He slowed his approach but still held the bat aloft and made slight movements toward getting at Derrick, who was whining and pulling his jacket off to get a look at his injured forearm.

"Fuckin' dog bit me!" he yelped and showed us the teeth marks smeared in blood.

"Stay outta my shit!" the shirtless fat man screamed, "or I'll let 'em off the chain and show ya what he can do!"

"Hey, take it easy." I waved my hands in front of his face to snap him out of the rage. "We're just looking for cars that were in an accident."

"Well, I ain't been in no accident. Get outta here!"

On a normal day, I'd have asked a few questions and gotten the ID of this guy who obviously had something to hide, probably drugs or an illegal firearm in the house, but he gets a free pass. His dog had done me a favor by stomaching the taste of such a foul piece of meat as Derrick Hinckle.

"Just go into the house. And get on the phone to schedule a tetanus shot," I said.

"I ain't payin' for no tetanus shot for that bozo!"

"No, not for him." I raised a hand to guide the man toward his home. "I mean for your dog. Who knows what viral shit that bozo's got."

The fat man allowed a slight snicker, then launched a few more verbal tirades at the brothers before heading back inside. The dog had taken a decent bite of Derrick, so I broke out the first-aid kit from my truck's glove compartment.

"You guys still want to go house to house?" I asked while cleaning the puncture wounds on his arm, "cause this is the nice neighborhood, and once we get to the slums, you'll have your hands full."

"Just hurry up," Dicky demanded.

"Ow!!!" Derrick growled. "Take it easy, man!"

"Dogs are the least of it. The folks in the rough patches got their kids all armed and ready to open fire on anybody snooping in the backyard."

Derrick winced as I yanked on the bandage to tie it off. "I'm gonna go shoot that dog,"

"You do that, and I'll have to shoot you."

"You just try it," Dicky warned. His eyes took on hostile slits, but glancing over my shoulder brought out a slight grin at the corners of his mouth. "Well, look-ee here."

After taking a cautious step back in case Dicky was trying to distract my attention so he could sock me a good one, I turned to see Ben's pickup roaring toward us. It slowed down to park behind mine, when it was clear to see that he wasn't alone in the cab.

Tammy was with him.

"What the hell?" I pushed Dicky aside and marched over to the passenger's side to rip the door open. "You all right? Get out of there!"

"Calm the fuck down, Sheriff," Ben laughed as Tammy

climbed out still dressed in a pair of flannel pants and oversized sweatshirt that she wore to bed. "I just brung you your lady."

"I'm OK. I asked him to take me to you." Tammy's words were meant to be reassuring but she was clearly nervous. "He came to the house. Barged right in and—"

"Look what I found!" Ben stepped out on the other side and held my old work laptop over his head. "Turns out the sheriff's got a backup computer!"

The whup-ass alarm clanging loudly in my head said to teach Ben a lesson in manners, but as I went after him, Tammy pulled my arm and halted my progress with her words.

"Cliff ran off."

"See, I gave my sister a call. She was nice enough to gimme your home address," Ben continued, "and somethin' she also said is your helpers at the station been workin' there long as she remembers. Said you're lyin' about havin' a new girl. And that lady you sicked us on earlier called you a liar, too. Then both you and your wife tell me you got no back up computer but shit, guess what? In about three seconds, I find a laptop marked *Rock Hollow Municipal* sittin' right on the kitchen counter. I gotta say that's a whole lot of lyin' for a lawman's family. Makes me think we should go take a good look in your neighborhood."

He paused and stared us both down. To her credit, Tammy simply locked her stare on him, tilted her head back and said nothing.

"Gonna need your password, Sheriff," Ben said harshly before moving to check in with his brothers, adding as he walked off, "I tried to coax it out your wife. Couldn't get nothin' outta her, charmin' as I am."

"Did that motherfucker put a hand on you?" I was one response away from taking on the three of them.

"No, he scared me, that's all. Came right into the house." She was shaking and leaned in with a whisper, "I didn't say anything but…did you get rid of the car?"

My whisper sounded more like a rasp. "Not yet."

"What the fuck, Blake?" she squealed.

"I've been busy!"

Sheriff, get over here," Ben called, placing down and flipping open the laptop on his truck's hood.

"Where'd Cliff go?" I leaned in, pretending to console Tammy with a hug.

"I don't know." Tammy was trembling all over, but she squeezed back. "We got into a fight when I got home. He said you told him that he didn't do it. Why did you say that?"

"I was trying to calm him down."

"Well, it didn't work!" She looked back at the brothers and then leaned into me. "I think he might be going to get the car himself."

"Perfect," I sighed, "just perfect."

"He's only trying to help."

"I've been asking him to mow the lawn for six years, and now he wants to help."

"Sheriff!" Ben shouted.

"Come here, boy!" Dicky added a couple of dog whistles.

"OK!" I shouted and then back to a whisper for Tammy, "Well, that's that. I'm past fed up with this bullshit, anyway."

When I took her by the arm and began leading her to the driver's side of my truck, Dicky took a few steps toward us and shouted.

"Where you think you're goin'?"

"I'm sending my wife back home, asshole," I shot back. "You never should've brought her."

"Hurry the hell up about it," Ben said and then added with a grind of his teeth, "asshole."

Dicky held his ground and Tammy got into the truck. I slammed the door shut before leaning in and taking her face to plant a big kiss on her startled lips. When I withdrew, we looked squarely at each other.

"I want you to pull away from here like you just robbed a bank. I'm going to jump in the back once you get going."

"Why?"

"To fire back at them when they start shooting," My answer made Tammy sit up rigid, but she started the engine right away.

"You fellas about ready?" I called out to the brothers, who looked like they were discussing potential sign-on words and numbers for the laptop, a practice that might go on until the next ice age.

"What's the password?" Ben's hands were ready to type.

"Let me see. Oh, yeah, it's 'fuck off, assholes.' Go! Go!"

Tammy hit the gas and tore off with such force that I almost missed hooking my arm over the side, causing my leap to be way off target. I slammed hard against the inside of the tailgate as a shot popped off and hit the back window near the passenger side, leaving a tiny hole and spider-web cracks in its wake. When I stuck my head up over the edge and prepared to fire in return, Ben was wrestling Dicky's arms down as another shot went off and hit the ground at their feet. Derrick was just standing there looking stupid, so as we hit the corner at the end of the street, I waved a middle finger. Derrick jolted to life and started chasing us at a full sprint while the other two headed for Ben's truck.

In addition to the two fabled certainties of life, death and taxes, I have had the misfortune of living under a third one, Tammy is the worst driver in the state and possibly the world. She flew out of there like a pro but took a chunk out of a minivan's bumper and obliterated the exterior mirror of a car on the other side of the street when executing the first tire-squealing corner. Even driving full-tilt down the straight quarter-mile road, she was pulling the steering wheel left and right, sending my flailing body careening around the bed as I tried to climb up to the back window.

"Hey! Hey!!" I shouted, gripping onto a hitch under the window and pounding on the glass. "Open up!"

Tammy had to slow down to take a narrow corner at the end of the road. After pulling around and speeding back up, she slid the window open.

"Where am I going?" she hollered.

"Take this left," I shouted over the whipping wind. When I checked on our pursuers, the brother's pickup was just taking a hard turn onto the road, not more than a quarter mile behind. "We gotta lead them outta town!"

People out on the sidewalks and yards gaped as the sheriff's truck flew by doing about eighty in a thirty zone, some perhaps even more curious to see the sheriff's wife at the wheel. One guy trying to get into his car had to dive across the hood to get out of the way. Tammy sure was owning the road in an awful way.

"I don't want to drive!" she shrieked.

"Well, I don't want to shoot nobody but I'm gonna have to unless you lose them!"

"Son-of-a-bitch!"

She hurled the truck around the corner at such speed that my grip came loose and I careened so hard into the side wheel-well that it knocked the wind out of me. Hard, tight pain hit my gut, and I fought to pull in a breath while crawling to get back to Tammy. Her searching face filled up the rearview mirror.

"I thought you fell over!"

I shook my head until a sip's worth of oxygen allowed me to get some strained words out. "Get off the bypass near the apple orchard."

The bypass is really just a big country dirt road, unchanged since the first loggers hauled horse-drawn wagons through these parts on their way south to Portland. As bad a driver as Tammy is, her knowledge of the terrain had the brothers beat. Although she struck a bullseye on a couple of deep potholes, one of which face-planted me and definitely loosened a tooth, for the most part she swerved around them. Also, Ben's monstrous pickup was delivering its occupants a few good jarring bumps that allowed us to pull away slightly and I silently sent out a big thank you to the town council for slashing the street department's budget.

After we got a safe distance from the town and temporarily out of the brothers' sight, I instructed Tammy take a sharp turn onto an old overgrown path leading to the river that folks only use for camping and fishing. Once we pulled behind a thick set of fir trees, I had her cut the motor and silenced us both with a finger pressed to my mouth. Like a quick answer to our prayers, Ben's truck approached loudly and roared past, trying to make up for the time they had lost in the pothole minefield.

"Let's give em a minute." I flipped myself over the passenger side of the truck, and only when hitting the ground did the damage from the wild ride set in. "Ah, fuck. Feels like you ran me over."

"Then you drive." Tammy blurted from inside the cab, finally able to let some anger conquer her fear. "We have to find Cliff."

"Not yet," I opened the passenger door and climbed in gingerly. "We gotta make sure they don't turn right around and…I need to just sit for a second."

"Oh, Blake," she said, softening, "you look like hell."

"I missed my beauty sleep." My eyes were closed before the words came out.

She let me have a few moments while we listened for the slightest sound of Ben's truck during a few tense moments but silence held strong. Even just a single wink of sleep would've' recharged my battery, but not with my wife around. Tammy has always been a talker.

"What do we do now?"

"Get outta trouble," I mumbled.

Instead of firing a sharp reply, Tammy sunk her head onto my shoulder. Suddenly we were that young couple once again, sneaking away from the world to catch hold of a cuddle in the woods.

"Thank you for giving up on arresting Cliff."

"Who said I have?" My body stiffened somewhat, but I left the shoulder still for her.

"I know you won't, cause you would've done it by now." She moved her head back so that her lips were up against my ear. "You love him more than anything."

"I love you both." It came out almost like an apology.

Tammy made a little groan and lifted her face up. Her soft cheek, once so familiar, felt strange against the stubble of my own.

Then she pressed her lips swiftly to mine, and it all felt so easy and nice, two rattled old lovers still giving off sparks for each other even under stressful pressure. We kept at it for a good half-minute. The moment was all wrong, but at least I was kissing the right woman for the first time today.

"I wish we had—"

She put a finger against my lips. "I'm through wishing."

"If Cliff gets found with that car…"

Tammy pulled back. "Right. Sure. I thought for a second, just a second, you were thinking about me."

"Tammy, don't. Not right now."

"When? When then?" She slapped my arm hard. "We're in this shit because of us! You and me."

"I want that kiss back."

"We brought all this on ourselves."

"Listen, Tammy," I said, lifting a hand up to rub my eyes. "I'm just trying to help our kid."

"What about me!" she shouted, instantly regretting the volume of her outburst. We sat for a few seconds in silence until the anger seeped into her whisper. "You can bet if I had killed that boy, you wouldn't help me."

"What the hell kind of thing is that to say?" I was once again amazed at how fast she can piss me off. "You are so selfish. This isn't about you."

"You wouldn't. It's the truth." She was scowling now. "Cause of Keith."

"Tammy, I swear," I responded grimly, "do not get me started on him."

"You hate me. Because we…You wanted to kill us both."

"God, Tammy."

She sat silently pissed off while I opened my door and slid out with a whole mix of anger and anxiety starting to at least take an edge off the pain in my hips and legs.

"Where are you going?" She was still mad, but the fear had returned to her face.

"They might've dropped one of them at the top of the road to catch us on the way out." I wanted to slam it hard but instead eased the door shut. "Basic military maneuver. So, you're going to stay here for a few more minutes while I backtrack through the woods."

"You're leaving me alone?"

"Just for a little bit." I looked out toward the road. "If that truck comes back, you just stay put. If it doesn't, then in exactly five minutes you pull outta here and tear toward town as fast as you did before. Pick me up on the bypass."

"Be careful."

"Ain't no such thing, darlin'," I drawled in my best cowboy accent. "Five minutes. Start counting now."

She said something else, but I hustled away too quickly to hear and was not sure I wanted to, anyway. To bring up Keith Griffin now, the woman for sure had more than one screw loose, never mind that I'd shot the guy dead earlier. I used my bitter mood to numb the pain in my thighs and back as I pushed through the woods at a jog. Hate is a strong term, though. She knew I hated Keith, he was the hating kind, but even though the two of us treat each other like it plenty, my wife and I don't hate each other. The kid figured into our staying together so long, but even if we split after all this madness, which seemed a severe likelihood, there would be a place inside me for Tammy, always. Wrecked people that try to patch each other up for a long time never let go of the first, violent attraction of discovering strange beauty in one another while wallowing at life's rock bottom.

"Fu-ck," I panted and almost stumbled coming down an overly rocky embankment.

The road appeared through a clear pocket between the spruce and fir trees. Trying to get my pounding heart to quiet, I slowed and got down onto my belly while still in protection of the woods. Crawling is not my favorite practice, making it an exhausting struggle to get through the tall grass that borders the bypass, waiting the whole time for a disturbed copperhead on the prowl to pounce and sink its sharp fangs into me.

Soon, I reached the fringe of the grass at the dirt and pebbles of the roadside, poking my head out slightly to see if there was anybody that might object to Tammy and I getting the hell out of here. I wiggled further out for a better look and, sure enough, Dicky Hinckle was about fifty yards down the road in the direction we needed to go, crouched behind a large boulder and a cluster of bare firebushes. For some reason, it's always the most unhinged and dangerous prick of the bunch that volunteers to cut off the escape route.

To add a gluey stickiness to the situation, I heard the far-off rumble of a truck approaching. Either Tammy was on her way, or Ben had double-timed it back down the mountain. No matter if it was a kill or rescue squad en route, Dicky needed to be taken care of immediately. But how? He was ready to fire off a long round of lead and metal and would waste no time putting one between my eyes at the first opportunity. Is he that low a scumbag to shoot a woman, though? More than probably. Even just the sight of Dicky with a gun in his hands will surely scare the hell out of Tammy and possibly run her off the road. The way she drove makes me imagine that she crashes a whole lot worse, and the lost cause of it all is if I even just winged one brother with a single bullet, it would set off a worse fire than the one already burning around this town.

As the roar of the truck grew closer, sneaky bastard Dicky began moving behind the rock in preparation to pounce on his prey. I kneeled up quickly, still covered by the high grass, and set myself like a track star awaiting the crack of the starter pistol. A sharp bend in the bypass guaranteed that neither Dicky nor I would know which ride was coming at us until after we were both out on the road.

The scream of the engine had almost reached the corner, and that's when Dicky made his move, lifting a leg over the rock with his gun drawn. Before he could swing the other leg over, I fired two shots into the ground in front of him. He slid himself backward and dropped out of sight, so I instantly took off as fast as a middle-aged, out of shape, variously injured son-of-a-bitch can run.

Like a raging fever, a mad plan blazed in my head. If it was Ben's truck, then I'd shoot a tire out and beat it back to the woods before Dicky shot me dead. A really terrible idea, but the only one I had. I took aim up the road, zigzagging in case Dicky had me in his sights. Then the sweet picture of my old, banged-up white F-150 barreling around the bend put an extra jolt into my dash.

Tammy bombed toward me, and I saw her strained face and crazed eyes behind the wheel as she slowed down, but I waved for her to keep going. Then, as if that clumsy attempt earlier was the only practice needed, I executed the perfect arm hook and upward leap into the bed of the truck, still landing hard but only one bad bounce this time. I rolled over, enjoying a slight moment of pride at a nimble display of athleticism that would've made any young lawman proud. I had only about two seconds to savor this slick and safe escape, when, as if dropped out of the clear blue sky, Dicky Hinckle suddenly landed on top of me.

The son-of-a-bitch felt like a duffel bag of dumbbells coming down on my back, and he started hammering punches to my neck and head. Tammy swerved wildly around a corner, and I managed to jerk loose and land a hard elbow to Dicky's cheek, which gave me enough space to roll over and get loose from his grip. It only made him madder, and he scrambled at me fast.

Despite taking a kick in the shoulder and a good wallop to the head, he somehow wrestled his way behind me and wrapped a strong and wiry arm around my neck. I gripped his other arm with both hands so he couldn't reach his gun, but the motherfucker was squeezing the air out of me. Kicking hard, I forced his leg to buckle. We both went down and almost tumbled out of the vehicle but he got me turned around and slammed my chest down so that my head hung over the tailgate and I watched the dust and rocks fly on the ground below us, while fighting hard not to join them.

Straining with all my might to hold on to his trigger hand, I had to pull him off somehow, but the pressure on my chest was painfully strong. As darkness began creeping across my eyes and my breathless gut jerked, at once both Dicky and I hurtled backward, feeling like the nightmare I was having was over and I was quite forcefully sucked back into reality.

Our bodies hit the rear wall of the cab with a force that could snap bones, but Dicky got caught between me and the metal tool chest, which he hit headfirst, instantly knocking him out cold. For a moment, I fought to get my throat to work again with struggling gasps and didn't even think about what the hell had just happened, then Tammy jumped out and reached over the side and I understood she had expertly stomped on the brakes of the truck, before Dicky could squeeze the life out of her husband.

Her hands were shaking when I took one. "Are you OK? I thought he was going to kill you!"

"So did he." I coughed and crawled over to open the back of the cab. "Help me get this piece of shit outta my truck."

Dragging the dirtbag out of the truck bed was easy enough but carrying him over to a nearby tree was a chore as fireworks of pain were popping off up and down and all over me and brought on a full body sweat. After checking to make sure he was still breathing, Tammy helped me prop him up against the trunk. She folded his arms over his belly so that he looked like he was simply taking an afternoon nap in the shade and close enough to the road so that his brothers wouldn't miss him on the way by.

"You, OK?" I asked Tammy after gingerly getting behind the steering wheel.

"No."

"Yeah, me neither." I spat some blood out of the window and swirled my tongue around to check for loose teeth. "All right, let's go."

"Where?" She gave me a lost look as I gunned the motor.

"We got to help Cliff get rid of that car so, like a lot of other doomed souls of Rock Hollow…We're going to the Maple Syrup Festival."

She returned my weak grin with a look of confusion. Under the circumstances, it was a whole lot better than fear and panic, although plenty of that was swimming around inside both of us.

After we got going, I reached my hand over and Tammy took it, squeezing hard and sliding herself closer to me. To show a little more spunk, she leaned forward and turned on the radio to whatever station was last left on. For the first time in many years, we tore across the back roads of town together, needing each other in a way that made us ache, while the song blasted through the speakers and thoroughly haunted our high-speed ride.

'Oh, mother, tell your children
Not to do what I have done
Spend your lives in sin and misery
In the House of the Rising Sun'

Chapter Eight

Festivals in their various shapes and forms have been a fabric of this tiny outpost, which is a mere freckle on the shoulder of our big-ass country, dating back to the times of the Native Americans, before the Europeans got here and fucked the place up. They had it right, the native folk. Their gatherings were celebrations of hunt or harvest in the spirit of giving thanks to the land that bestowed such bounty prior to the long, hard winters. Or after the days and nights of ice and snow had passed, individuals, tribes, and nations alike celebrated the returning bounties from springtime streams and fields.

The early festivals that the first nations of Rock Hollow threw bore no resemblance to the self-indulgent affairs stuffed into the calendar by the current town organizers, where they sit back and record any social faux pas committed by so-called friends and rivals, such as so-and-so's spouse having too much to drink or his or her significant other doing some grab-assing out of wedlock, stocked ammunition for brutal gossip later on. The celebrations of nature or holidays are mere fronts to test their neighbors on cliquish societal proving grounds that unfold much like dinner parties thrown by vampires, where guests are famously wined and dined, but by the end a bunch of unlucky souls always end up with life sucked out of them.

If you could name the most destructive element that the Europeans introduced to North America, aside from the obvious hate, greed, and cruelty, then it would be vanity. The settlers came and saw the native people praising the environment for their thriving existence but in their minds no individual should have a better time with life than the white man, so they put a stop to it with religion and commerce and other blighting practices of those first continental party-poopers.

Not to say that in our current age the folks in charge of Rock Hollow don't know how to throw a party, because no season passes without one. Even the Midwinter Shindig coaxes townsfolk, buried under three feet of snow and terrorized by wind chills well below zero, to crawl out of their homes for a few hours of singsongs while getting completely pie-eyed on heavily spiked punch. A great many attendees are not seen nor heard from for several days but once recovered most agree that even a single night of stupid fun can help folks who have gone nearly mad with cabin fever to remember what it was like to be human for a short while, and that can go a long way in the middle of a snowy northern New England winter.

So, even though the Maple Syrup festival is one of a string of events that Lydia stages throughout the year to make a big cash profit for her country club, which then reports staggering losses from each community affair on her tax returns, the big allure is still the timing of spring awakening. This allows the Rock Hollow community to come together and give a proper—and expensive, if you're not a club member— welcome to the approaching spring after a bitterly cold, snowbound winter, which always seems to be just one approaching cold front from returning throughout the month of April. In Rock Hollow, folks will advise that even though Red Sox games are back on the radio and the light green buds are popping out on the trees, it still gets down into the low thirties at night. There have been numerous occasions in the past when the festival grounds had to be plowed after a surprise early spring blizzard, and attendees not only had to contend with a loss of equilibrium from ten-dollar shots of eighty proof maple syrup vodka, but also the slippery patches of ice underfoot.

But not this spring. The weather is clear, and the air is crisp. Once we'd driven up onto Pure Gold Road, which Lydia badgered the town to rename from the humble original moniker, Wild

Goat's Path, we discovered that despite its snobbish style and reputation, today's festival was going to achieve record attendance. The traffic was backed up a long way from where the road enters the woods and it's another half mile up to the club's entrance. Cars weren't budging, and many vehicles were simply parked off-road, their occupants choosing a short hike up the mountain to over an hour-long wait for parking.

"Geez," Tammy said as we neared the line of cars, "Lydia sure knows how to throw a party."

"Oh, yeah. The best of the best will be here today."

"I don't think we're dressed for the occasion." Tammy shook her head a little, impressively clinging to social proprieties while shit was raining down in buckets around us.

"You look stunning."

"You don't," she chuckled, and I had to swat her hand aside as she tried to wipe my face with her sleeve.

I eased the truck off the road, onto a pitched embankment where no owner of a $100,000 BMW or Lexus had dared park, and we began walking to the club, along with some other far more coiffed and primped citizens on their own stroll. Tammy clutched my arm as we passed into the shade of the woods where the road climbs upward, and I did my best to pull her along while pretending that every bone in my body wasn't killing me. The line of idling vehicles stretched all the way up the narrow road and after passing about thirty of them, we neared the small meadow they call the parking area, which was chock-full. Of course, Lydia saved money by not hiring an attendant to bring some order to the mess.

When we passed a nice-looking Cadillac with its fine motor purring away near the front of the long line, the window slid down and a hand reached out.

"Sheriff," came the deep, sandpapery voice of John Camponelli, "the hell is the holdup here?"

John has a firm grip on the home oil delivery contracts for about a fifty-mile radius. He's likely the richest man in the county, who has donated tons of money into the municipal funds to maintain roads and repair bridges, although many say it's only to keep a clear path for his trucks to pump oil into homes, several of which have had their flow of Texas Tea cut off in the middle of harsh temperatures because they didn't pay their bills. John and I aren't friends but have grown to like each other and his occupying the third seat on the Town Board has saved my ass from Lydia's wrath many times.

When he leaned out of the car, Tammy kept moving but I stepped back to shake his hand.

"Hey-a John."

His two youngsters were in the back, arguing with each other while simultaneously staring at tablets on their laps. His wife, Loretta, nice enough although she takes zero interest in anything other than tennis and money, had the sun shield down and was touching up her face in the small mirror.

"The fuck they doing up there squirting maple syrup up people's asses before you can get in? Kids, will you pipe down! Loretta, say hi to the sheriff."

"Hi, Sheriff," Loretta said stiffly as she applied lipstick.

I looked back at Tammy, who was hurrying me along with her eyes.

"Come on, always with the face," John scolded his wife before jutting his head out to me, his jet-black hair slicked plentifully with what looked to be a derivative of his home-heating product, expertly covering his bald spot. After squinting at me with tired brown eyes, half-ringed with dark circles, he furrowed his brow.

"Jesus Christ, Blake. You look like you got run over by a horse. A fucking Clydesdale."

"Yeh. I got some crazy brothers of—"

"I know the deal," A grim look came over his face. "Lydia said she wants to shitcan you. Kids, enough! Pipe down or the tablets go! I swear to fucking…"

"Don't say it!" His wife smacked him hard on the shoulder, and they all argued for about fifteen seconds before Loretta went back to her makeup and the kids to their tablets.

"For fuck's sake." He turned back to me. "You know, Lydia and Pyles can do it without me. Two to one."

"I appreciate the warning, John," I replied, tapping the top of his car, "but it's really the least of my problems right now."

"I mean if you can close that hit-and-run situation," John said under his breath, "*then* I got something to argue with them about. I can bend that piece of shit Pyles but you gotta give me—."

"I'll keep doing my job til it ain't mine anymore."

I turned to join Tammy, and John shouted after me as I moved away.

"Just know that I think you're all right. Always did. If you need me to get you work or maybe a good lawyer to scratch out a settlement with the town, you call me."

"Blake…" Tammy likely wanted to shout, but she managed to coo my name.

"Appreciate it, John." I raised a hand in farewell.

"Do me a favor," John called one last time. "Have them send somebody down here to sit in my car. Tell him it's a hundred bucks and my good graces."

Giving him a thumbs up, I thought how much I'd have loved to sit in his warmed-up Caddy right now. A hundred bucks would certainly pay the piper but hell I would've done it for free.

Tammy pulled close to me again as soon as we started off. "That's the oil guy, right?"

"Yep, and a councilman."

"He said you're going to be fired. Is that true?"

"I don't know." I should have looked her squarely in the eye, but I couldn't. "Maybe. Almost wish they would."

Tammy guided me away from the other folks moving uphill, a few of whom I could tell wanted to ask me for an update on either the hit-and-run or the short-lived takeover of the bakery this morning. I scowled meanly to ward off any potential interlocutors and was about to remind Tammy that we were running out of precious time to find either the car or Cliff but she spoke first.

"Let's go."

"We're going," I replied, giving her hand a tug, "come on."

She tugged back. "I mean after we find Cliff. Let's get out of here. Run away to someplace else."

"Are you nuts?" I muttered playfully as if she had cracked a joke but then realized she was dead serious. "My job. The house. How's a kid supposed to go to college if—"

"We could! Empty the bank accounts. Give the house to my mom somehow. We could…" Her eyes were searching the woods for answers that weren't there. "We could go to New York or Florida or…"

I brought my face close to hers. "Tammy, we can't."

Whether it had been truly a spark of hope or just frantic dreaming, the wide, wishing eyes lost their light and her visage melted into a bitter scowl.

"You just don't fucking care," Now, her voice had a deep loathing in it. "You never, ever did."

"Listen, I'm doing all that I can," I said softly while leading us back to the path, "but we've got to find him first. Then—"

"Say, Sheriff," inquired a middle-aged man, a teacher at the elementary school in nearby Marbleton. "What was that all about at the bakery this morning?"

I whipped my cell phone out and stuck it to my ear, "Sorry. On an important call."

The man had his arm draped around his skinny wife, who turned and pointed at Tammy.

"It's Tanya, right?" she twirled the finger lazily, dangerously unaware of how combustible my wife was at the moment. "Do you know what it was about?"

"Take out your cell, pretend it's an emergency" I instructed Tammy quietly, then shouted into my phone and breezed past the couple. "Well, geez-Louise, that's no answer! I want answers!"

"No," Tammy barked at her phantom caller, keeping right on my heels, "that's not going to work! No, no, no, no, no!"

We scurried up the road, putting a silencing hand up to the few intruders who dared to interrupt our engrossing yet fake phone calls. At last, we reached the gates of the club, where folks in a big, uneven line were waiting to pay the admission fee.

Although tempted to go the long way around and avoid the crowd, I knew that the old logging road that Tammy had found ran almost directly behind *Pure Gold* and according to her estimate, the car would be just a short way up the mountain. Unfortunately, that meant the quickest route by far is straight through the belly of the festival-beast.

"C'mon. We gotta go in."

We marched straight to the front of the line where a young man dressed like a sort of stylish lumberjack was taking cash and dispensing tickets at a white folding table next to the entry gate.

"Hi," I said with a smile as we stepped up to the wannabe Paul Bunyan and cut off the next party in line, "I'm here on sheriff's office business, so my deputy and I will be going in."

"They didn't mention anything to me. I'll call Lydia."

He pulled his phone out in a flash, so I reached over and snatched it from his hand.

"Hey!"

"Did you hear the words 'sheriff's business'? Lydia knows all about it. In fact, how do you know I'm not here to keep an eye on you?"

My tone reminded me of TV cops, cynical and fake, but the faux-lumberjack's face went blank, signifying either some kind of guilt or ignorance or both. I tossed the phone back to him and took Tammy's hand, leading us into the large and meandering Maple Syrup crowd.

"I'm still going to call Lydia," he whined as we moved away.

"By all means. I call her all kinds of things every day," I bellowed as we marched off. "It's sort of like scream therapy."

In another time and under severely different circumstances, this afternoon out with the wife would've been a rare and pleasant occasion, walking together through a spring festival with all the time in the world. The weather beckoned us to stay and hob-nob with gorgeously bright sunshine, cold but delicious air that might touch fifty degrees come the late afternoon. Instead, we kept heads down in a hasty, snaking journey through the large pockets of people, cutting off any chatty townsperson's attempted conversation with a quick hand in the air and a look to kill, and moving with purpose while avoiding larger groups around the hard cider and wine stations.

When we passed by a small row of canopies set up to hawk grossly expensive jewelry, designer clothing, and sunglasses, I snatched up a cashmere sweater for us to both hide our faces, barely avoiding Melvin Pyles as he roamed around glad-handing anyone who welcomed it. We only had to ignore a few more folks calling out to us, one being an old woman who clumsily caught the purloined sweater after I lobbed it her way, and soon arrived at the food tents, which, along with the dining area, were backed up against the tennis courts at the rear of the property.

We hustled and excused ourselves through the many lines of folks seeking goodies such as pancakes with fresh maple syrup, maple fudge, and maple pudding. Now, all we needed to do was slip into the woods behind the courts, and our great escape is complete, with under a mile's trudge straight uphill left to reach…

The moment we turned to cut past the dining area and get to the courts, guess who in the fucking world appeared, seated directly in front of us in the VIP area at a picnic table piled high with food? None other than the host of my nightmares, Lydia the Poison Frog.

"Oh, shit," Tammy said under her breath.

"Indeed," I whispered.

"What in God's name happened to you?" Lydia forced a large mouthful of pancake down in between words laced with condescension. "You have a *lot* of explaining to do, mister."

She and her guests were seated at the largest picnic table, of course, which was crammed with the culinary treats of the day: loads of pancakes, tons of maple fudge and several large mixing bowls filled to the top with maple pudding. Joining her at the feast was her husband, Charles, an easy-to-forget man who has looked to be in his late-fifties since he was twenty. By now, he probably was, and to meet him is to walk away amazed how anyone can go on living each day with such a horrible woman.

Living proof of their hideous union, a boy of tween years with hippie-length brown hair was sitting between Lydia and Charles. Young Simeone, nicknamed Simmie, was of portly build, obviously culled by following the dietary guidelines of his mother, making one wonder, as Charles was lean, if mother and son leave nothing on the table for him after they've had their share. At the moment, Simmie was captivated with one of the large bowls of pudding, of which he had eaten half and was a sure bet to finish.

A younger couple was also seated at the table, Bob and Penny Biddle, who ran a mail order vitamin business out of their palatial mountain home. One would wonder how nutrition tablets could fund such a lavish lifestyle until you learn the vitamins come from Mexico, as do the much stronger, off-market, mind-expanding supplements that their many customers order in bunches. The joke about town is that the Biddle's business is continually "mushrooming."

"Oh my gosh, Sheriff," Bob said with a look of guarded wonder that can only come from a fully glazed mind. "You're like…bleeding, man."

"Everybody keeps telling me that, but I say it's a rumor." I smiled and took a quick bow. "Now if you'll excuse us…"

Tammy had been hiding behind me the whole time, and when I turned to take us out of there, we momentarily got tangled and looked like a couple of circus clowns drumming up laughs.

"Is that the man you're gonna fire, Mamma?" Simmie blurted loudly and then followed it up with a wet pudding belch.

I saw the look of fury rush onto Tammy's face and shook my head vigorously. We might have managed to pull away free if Lydia had not snapped her reply quicker than I could haul my wife away.

"Yup, that's the incompetent fool I'm going to fire," she shouted loud enough for the other tables to take notice, as if the arrival of the banged up and bleeding sheriff hadn't done that already. "Calls himself a lawman but he can't uphold the law. In my opinion, he isn't much of a man either."

I made one last tug on Tammy's hand, but it would've been easier trying to hold back the ocean with a broom.

"You fat, spoiled, clueless, ugly windbag!" Tammy roared.

The animal was out of the cage, and the collective response from the group was wide-mouthed shock, including Simmie, who still had his own stuffed with pudding. Against all better judgment, I released Tammy's hand so she could knock over the sandwich board that read "VIP Seating" and march right up to the table.

While husband, child, and friends cowered, Lydia reached her big face forward with the smuggest frown she could muster, goading Tammy on as if she needed any more influence.

"You call yourself the boss of this town? Why do half the kids live below the poverty level? You'd think a town manager could handle the safety and welfare of a thousand people, but oh no, you let kids starve!"

Out of shame or maybe just due to a bulging gut stuffed to near-exploding, Simmie stopped devouring the pudding.

"No-brains, loud-mouthed Tammy Buskin," Lydia hissed. "Can't take her anywhere. Here's some fashion advice, girlfriend. You are *way* underdressed."

Tammy isn't the type to let shithead digs like that get to her, and she judges words based on the quality of the person delivering them, which I admire. But she had recently walked six miles to get out of the freezing cold woods, got shot at by degenerates, and had nearly killed us both more than once with her courageous yet awful driving skills. That, combined with desperate shame and guilt over Cliff's situation, had pushed her patience level into the red. I gladly stood back and watched her pick up Simmie's massive bowl of pudding and throw a giant, splattering handful of sugary goop into Lydia's face.

"You!" Lydia kicked her chair back and stood with arms extended, seemingly monosyllabic for the first time since I've known her. "You!"

"*You* are a horrible, ugly slug!" Tammy shouted, having no enunciation problems whatsoever, "and you can't cover ugly up with money!"

Lydia, looking like a Hershey bar had exploded in her face, emitted a weird, strangled growl like a wolf choking on a whole chicken as she tried to dive over the table with outstretched arms to get to Tammy.

Acting perhaps a little too late, but worth the delay, I grabbed Tammy's shoulder and pulled her away. The wild attempt to seize her enemy had only earned Lydia a hard landing onto a plate of maple fudge, which was now smeared across her massive yellow parka. As soon as Lydia landed on the table, Penny Biddle burst into shroom-induced, seal-like barks of laughter, which instantly infected Bob. While we backed away, the Biddle's were falling upon each other in a merry fit.

Charles stood up and clawed his wife back to her feet, where she struggled to get her mussed hair in order, picking pieces of fudge from between her breasts and screaming at the top of her lungs.

"You're fired! I want your badge! Now! Now! NOW!"

"Until it goes to a vote," I instructed with a good dose of mockery, "only the judge can take my badge."

"I'm right here." Judge Prowse stood up slowly from a nearby table. "I think we'd better have a talk, Sheriff."

"It's a bad time," I replied, "I've got to—"

"Give me your badge!" Lydia was now circling towards us, an irate and food-stained spectacle. "Give it to me!"

Tammy and I didn't need to say a word to each other. We ran away holding hands like two naughty school kids. For the first time in days, the rush of something other than gloom arose, bringing a rush of warmth to my chest as we waded into the large crowd near the food tents. I even helped myself to a steaming pancake from a plate that was waiting to be sold, nodding in thanks to the woman behind the checkout table, who admonished me but then shrugged it off.

"We gotta go back where we came in," I mumbled to Tammy while inhaling the pancake, wishing I'd grabbed two. "Follow me."

At the back of the pancake tent, there were stacks of large canisters that had been emptied of maple syrup, so I gave one to Tammy and grabbed one myself. She followed my lead, hoisting the drum on her shoulder and switching hands to get used to the cold, sticky metal, and then we headed toward the front gate like a couple of festival workers.

The enduring problem of the small town that never, ever gets out of your fucking business persisted when Tom Dillon, an acquaintance that I hunt with occasionally, caught my eye and blocked our path with his tall, beefy frame. He was carrying two large steins of hard cider and with flushed cheeks, gleaming eyes, and dampened whiskers at the edge of his mustache, he looked to have knocked back at least twice that many already,

"Blake! How the hell are ya!" he roared.

I could hear Lydia's shouts approaching from behind and wanted to shove Tom aside, but he was too good of a guy to knock around. Still, he wouldn't shut up.

"Is that the missus there?" he went on, peaking his head around me before busting into a belly-laugh. "What are you two doin'? Makin' off with a year's supply of syrup?"

"Come here, pal!"

I dropped the cannister and grabbed Tom into a bear hug, turning him between me and the sound of Lydia's approaching howls while Tammy slid behind the both of us.

"Easy, son," Tom chuckled and pushed himself from my grip, "I don't hug the boys. You know that."

"Do me this favor and I'll have two bottles of scotch at your house tomorrow." I looked Tom dead in the eye.

"You name it."

"I need you to tie up Lydia Bernard. Tell her…tell her there are rats in the pancake tent."

Tom was the perfect man for this kind of job. On many a Saturday night, *The Deuce* could not legitimately close at 3 o'clock in the AM without Tom standing up on a chair and belting out "Rocky Road to Dublin".

Tom chewed happily on the challenge, "Rats, huh? OK, will do. Make it Johnnie Walker Black. So long, kids!"

He stalked off in search of Lydia while Tammy and I took cover in yet another tent laden with expensive items. This one held a wide selection of the type of oversized cups with straw tops that keep beverages hot or cold and most times are carried by middle-aged and older ladies who've finally found a safe way to drink wine in public before noon.

"What are we doing?"

"We don't need Lydia chasing us out of the gate. So, let's hold on a second. Catch our breath."

"Yeah, it's been one fuck of a day," a deep voice said from behind me.

Something hard dug into my back, and even with my winter coat on, I knew the end of a gun barrel when I felt one. Tammy turned around, and her eyes got big. The voice belonged to Ben Hinckle.

"You're runnin' away from everybody today, Sheriff," Ben remarked and dug the barrel of the gun deeper into me.

Tammy started backing away but Ben stopped her with a harsh, whispered command. "You stay put or I will take your man out to the woods and blow his fuckin' head off. Shoulda done it years ago."

She stopped and looked around the tent. A few ladies were perusing the wares while the young girl responsible for checking folks out was half-asleep in a lawn chair.

"We got into that computer, Sheriff." Ben pulled me back to the corner of the tent, and Tammy followed. Once we got there, he stripped the firearm out of my holster. "My sister told us where your day-dispatcher lives. That Barbara is one fuckin' ornery bitch and her husband put up a pretty good fight, but once Derrick broke the guy's arm, she fired that computer right up for us."

"You fucking pricks," I panted.

"Yeah, that's us," Ben laughed, "and these fucking pricks found something out. There's a black sedan registered to your house."

"So, what," I was playing his game for now.

Tammy couldn't help but participate. "There are hundreds of cars in this town, asshole."

"Tell your scrawny bitch to shut the fuck up," Ben snapped and jammed the barrel hard into my kidney.

"Uh, Tammy," I winced and held a finger up, "do not argue with a sick mind."

"Now I ain't no genius but with the way you been actin' and the fact you got the kind of car we're lookin' for…I figure you either take me to it and we settle things like gentlemen, or we can see what the folks out there think we should do."

"You'll end up looking like a fool. We don't know anything," I laughed.

"Let's find out." He pushed me hard, and I pitched forward, almost stumbling into a woman deciding between a hot pink or putrid purple cup.

"Keep your hands off him!" Tammy hissed and took a step towards us.

"No, Tam." I put myself between her and Ben. "Let's just go."

We marched out of the tent with Ben hardly a step behind. The girl at the front woke up and gave us a tired smile. I figured maybe we could just run for it and Ben wouldn't have the nerve to start shooting in the middle of a crowd, but before I could calculate the chances of his restraint or even which way to go, Lydia let out an angry screech from the opposite side of the line leading into the pancake tent.

"There he is! Judge, I found him! Get his badge!"

I eyeballed Tammy for her to make a run toward the gate but she did not look like one prepared for a risky escape. Her face had gone pale and she shook her head at me.

Just as I nodded my head in the affirmative, Tom Dillon's voice cut far above the din of festival goer chatter and classical music coming from speakers in the windows of the main house.

"There are rats in the pancake tent! Rats! In the pancake tent! Rats!"

A brief hush fell over the large group of folks in and around the tent until Tom screamed out the last lines of his gracious performance with blood-curdling gusto.

"In the pancake tent! I just got *bit* by a BIG POISON RAT!! They're EVERYWHERE!!"

Patrons began shouting, cursing, and pouring out of the newly christened rats' nest, some with loaded plates still in hand, others tossing them aside as if holding food made them targets of the sudden infestation. The fleeing crowd bumping frantically into the many people mulling about outside of the tent created a confused and raucous melee of panicked noise.

"Go!" I took hold of Tammy, shouting and jamming the keys in her hand. "Get to the safe place! Now!"

I tried pushing her along, but Ben yanked me hard from behind. Tammy showed that there was plenty of courage left in her as she snatched the keys and bolted away, bouncing off a few folks fleeing imaginary vermin, then disappearing out of sight.

Ben hammered a fist into the back of my neck.

"Son-of-a-bitch! Tell me what your hidin'!"

"All right!" I turned my head toward him, "I confess, I love disco! Ah-ah-ah-ah stayin' alive! Stayin'—"

"Enough of this shit." Ben held tight to my jacket and lifted the gun from my midsection, firing three successive shots into the air.

Rats in their pancakes had whipped the crowd into a frenzy already, but the reaction to the gunshots was pandemonium. Everyone either hugged the ground or made tracks to dive behind tents, upended display tables, or each other, in a kind of panic that would've kept spreading if Ben hadn't screamed for quiet, adding one more shot in the air for emphasis. Of course, none of the brave members of the country club tried to disarm him as he jammed the gun into my shoulder blades.

"Everybody shut up! Shut up! I got something to say!" Ben hollered.

The added bullet blast did nothing to calm people down but the sight of the gun pointed in a single direction seemed to allay nerves. Folks felt safe if it was only the sheriff in danger, and hell, they could always get another one of them.

Surprisingly, Melvin Pyles, displaying balls that I never knew he had, stepped into the large space that people had cleared around Ben and myself. He stretched a calming hand out while also ducking his head slightly.

"Hey, ah…now…." he tripped over his words and an abandoned backpack on the ground before continuing, "you're one of the Hinckle boys, right?

"Shut up!" Ben spat. "Your sheriff is hidin' somethin' and I'm bettin' it's got to do with my dead nephew!"

"OK, OK," Melvin coddled nervously while glancing at the folks peeking out from their hiding places. "We can talk about that. Just—"

"I am talkin' bout it!" Ben roared. "Ever since I got to town your lawman has been lyin' and runnin' away from everybody. Somethin' stinks!"

Lydia's crow-like wail came from somewhere far off. "Take his badge!"

My temper was making a remarkable comeback as I shook free from Ben's grip and turned to him.

"This man is crazy! He's been causing trouble since he got to town!"

Tom Dillon and another guy were creeping along about twenty paces behind Ben. If he kept blabbing for another minute, maybe we'd get a chance to jump and disarm him.

"Where's his car, huh?" Ben went on, and the people lying on the ground nearby began giving me suspicious looks as if this were nothing more than a political debate, one that I was losing. "This man is hidin' something. Where's his car?"

"I don't know," I gasped, holding my hands outward in

feigned confusion. "It's gone missing. We think it might've been stolen."

"He's lyin'!" Ben shook with anger and pointed the gun at my face as the crowd let out gasps and squeals.

"I swear on all that's holy," I shouted to the sky like a backwoods preacher, "my family is innocent!"

Being an individual who prefers agnosticism but is forever tied to some kind of faith inside, the response that came seconds after my proclamation suggested I had finally pissed off the Almighty for the last time. A rumble started some way off but gained in proximity. A hissing squeal joined it, and everyone turned toward the dining section, which was empty now except for the many tables laden with food. The rumble transformed into a roar. If it had kept approaching for another second or two, I would've clubbed Ben one good in the head with one of the many empty cider steins littering the ground.

Before I could make a move to grab hold of one, everybody's attention was drawn beyond the dining area to the tennis courts and a car emerging from the woods at high speed. When it took out a line of shrubs and an old picnic table, it almost seemed like some kind of armored beast. It did not swerve or veer until it smashed straight through the chain-link fence on far side of the court, then flew across and took out the netting on the way to smashing into the opposite fence.

When people began swarming to get out of its way, I realized it was Tammy's car that she had dumped in the woods. Maybe Ben did too because he turned to me with a look of amazement across his face, right before an enormous woman barreled into him and his grip on my jacket ripped away. He also dropped my gun which had been tucked in the waistband of his pants and I scooped it up and started moving, unsure where to head next.

The out-of-control car, dragging a section of fence behind it, careened into an abandoned wagon display of jewelry as it touched onto the open grass, spun wildly and then started coming straight towards me. A strange mix of anger, disgust and pride filled me at the sight of Cliff behind the wheel. He looked scared but in charge, so I turned and ran off toward the croquet courts at the front of the club grounds, which are always unplayable and unoccupied until June because of the mass of migrating geese that shit all over them during their short visits.

No one appeared to follow except for Cliff, who had somehow avoided every terrified person in his path, although he destroyed a table laden with arts and crafts when he swung the vehicle in my direction. In some distant corner of my mind, I thought about the auto insurance policy hikes mounting up.

As expected, the geese were having a poop-party on the ten-acre swath of grass reserved for junior and adult croquet. A large flock lurched into the air when I sprinted toward them but I ducked out of their way and promptly slid across the wet, shitty lawn, struggling back to my feet in time to jump awkwardly to the side, as Cliff hit the brakes and skidded to a stop.

"Get in!"

He was a nervous wreck, staring into the rearview mirror. I hurried to the driver's side and yanked the door open.

"Push over!"

"No! Just get in!" he shouted back, looking as crazy as I felt.

"Damn it, push over!"

"You never let me drive!" he barked and slammed the steering wheel.

A shot rang out, and a bullet careened off the top of the car. Now, Cliff let me shove him over, and I caught sight of Ben on the far side of the field running toward us, reloading his gun. My foot was on the accelerator even before I was fully inside the car, and we took off toward the electric deer fencing that enveloped the grounds.

I pushed Cliff's head down seconds before Ben got two more shots off at us. One missed, and the other might have lodged in the body near the trunk. The motherfucker was shooting at the gas tank!

After mowing down some decorative bushes, we both braced

ourselves as the car smashed through the high-tensile wire barricade and began bouncing into the woods, leaving that son-of-a-bitch to explain his side of the story to the country club crowd.

"You were…supposed to dump it…in the gorge." My words were breathless and interspersed as I fought to steer around boulders and trees.

"I couldn't…get up there." With nothing to hold onto but the overhead grab handle, Cliff was being tossed about. "So, I parked it…behind the club. I was gonna…oomph…wait until dark, but…that guy was gonna shoot you!"

"Maybe. Maybe not." I winced as we narrowly missed one tree while swerving around another but managed to shoot a warm look at Cliff. "Thank you, though."

"You're welcome," he beamed with pride before knocking his head on the roof as we hit a huge bump.

After slowing down to carefully navigate a dry gulley, we hit a marshy open field that took a few minutes to cross, with one anxious moment of tires spinning uselessly in the fresh spring mud. Like a true woodsman, Cliff leapt out of the car, stripped his jacket off and laid it under the stuck tire. After a couple of pushes, we broke free of the pit.

When he jumped back into the car, he was still clutching the mud-caked jacket.

I pointed at it as I navigated the car onto the road near the end of the long line of festival cars reaching into the woods. "Are you serious?"

"It's a good jacket," he replied, hugging it to his abdomen.

A cursory check of the rearview confirmed that no one was following and the mayhem behind us at the club had surely kept Ben from giving chase for a while. I soon turned us onto the bypass, heading toward town. By now, I was light years past exhaustion, and the knocks and bruises were no longer numbed by adrenaline. This old, hurt body needed a long soak in a tub of steaming water and salts, but the day's events certainly weren't over, not by a long shot.

"Where we going?" Cliff piped up once we had driven further away from the club.

I looked over at my son and gave him an emotionless stare. There was no other way to do it.

"Sorry, kid. I gotta take you to jail."

Chapter Nine

You…you're gonna…" Cliff's shaky voice trailed off as he stared down at his lap, looking like a dismayed little boy and striking me with a harsher sorrow than he knew.

"Just for now." The words came out hard and choked at first, but the kid needed strength to survive this mess, so I hammered on, "I'm gonna lock you in the cell and keep guard at the door with a shotgun till the staties get here. Then we're going to work this thing out."

We rode along in silence while the car paid us back for its recent labor in the wilderness obstacle course. Blasts of cold air rushed through massive cracks and dents in the body, as well as a partial missing piece of the floorboard, revealing the ground whizzing by under our feet. The heating system was unresponsive despite some frustrated pounding of my fist onto the console, so we resigned ourselves to a frigid trip.

"Don't worry," I said, placing my free hand on Cliff's shoulder, "we're gonna get through this."

He looked at me sadly but at this point there was really nothing I could do to improve the situation. After his destructive spin around the country club, combined with whatever shit Ben Hinckle is blabbing to anybody who'll listen, the cat was out of the bag and about to scratch our eyes out. Still, I saw it clearly written on his drained face he had been holding out with a last hope that his dad would somehow save him.

"I don't have any magic words that can make all this hurt go away," I leaned toward him as I continued, having to console in a shout over the blasts of air and the clobbered, whining engine, "but just like the family of that boy are gonna have to find a way to heal…to keep on going. Same goes for us. We're gonna take our punishment together and get to the other side."

They were the last words spoken during the rest of the ride back into town. Still, the temptation was strong to pull over and ask Cliff to drive, because my eyes were blurring and a pounding headache had engulfed my skull, like my brain wanted to come out and play. Things had run at such a hellish pace in the last bunch of hours that the pause of a wordless flight along this empty back road with the sun casting a bright April shine, and the sky as blue as a pope's robe, carried the odd sense I wasn't a part of this world. Somehow, I'd been picked up and dropped into another Rock Hollow that existed in a parallel dimension, like in the old sci-fi movies and comic books from the 1950s. I'm still me, but nobody else is themselves because the aliens got them. Or maybe they're all destined to become aliens and I'm the only one who's different and…

"I need a nap," I said, shaking my head hard to regain focus.

"You sort of…look like you need a doctor."

"Nah, just a first aid kit and a bartender."

Cliff laughed a little, and I did, too, both of us searching for anything to keep the gloom away. Finally, we got to the fringe of town, and I slowed our speed so we could get a couple of things straight.

"Don't be afraid, OK? Shit happens and the better you stand up to it the easier it will be to live your life later on. Trust me."

"OK."

As we cut through neighborhoods to get to Main Street, folks were out enjoying their Sunday, youngsters playing in yards, adults raking leaves they'd never got to before last year's first good snow. The image of normalcy brought a wave of envy, and I bit my lip as we slowed down and waited for some kids to clear their kickball game out of the way. The group reluctantly filed onto the sidewalk and gawked at our beat-up vehicle, so I gave them a friendly wave as we took off. Don't try this at home, kids!

Cliff was watching them, too, and probably wishing he was ten years old again, with nothing to do but play outside before being called home to a hot meal.

"Your life will go on, Son," I assured him. "All this shit is going to be a detour, nothing but a long way around to get to where you're supposed to be."

We had taken the side street route through town, because there was no need to run into the other two Hinckle brothers before safely getting Cliff under lock and key. When we turned one final corner, a most welcome sight won the "best fucking thing that's happened all day" award— a state police cruiser sitting outside the station. Finally, dear God, we'd caught a break. Even though it meant the first step of Cliff's rough path through the legal system was going to come far sooner than I'd like. Maybe our simply deciding to do the right thing had caused our bad luck to run out.

I pulled past the cruiser and neared a small group of people chatting in front of the entrance. Two state police officers were facing the building opposite a young couple, one male, one female. The young man and I made direct eye contact, leaving me no doubt that they were the two hikers from the trouble at Keith's place. Just like that, bad luck had come roaring back.

The tires squealed angrily as I tore away with a sudden speed that jerked Cliff back in his seat. The harsh rattle of the engine and a funneling cloud of black smoke coughed from the banged-up muffler to further highlight our ignominious departure. In the rearview mirror, I watched the two staties turning to assess the commotion, one of them taking some steps toward the street and waving the mist of exhaust from his face. Because my internal magnet of misfortune would not let up, I abandoned Main Street and tore down a couple of side lanes, then pulled the car over real fast and started pushing at Cliff's shoulder.

"Get out. Hurry up! Out!"

He unbuckled quickly but didn't make a move for the door. "What's happening?"

"I need you to get to the safe place. Your mum will be there."

"Wh-what will you—"

"Get out!" My temples almost burst with the force of my demand.

Cliff almost jumped out of his skin, then jerked the door open and hurried out onto the sidewalk. Still, he bent down and looked at me desperately.

"Please, kid, go to the safe place. I love you. It will be OK. Just please, run!"

He started walking. Although there were no cop sirens in the air or pickups in hot pursuit, they would certainly be on their way. Those staties will eventually answer the flurry of calls that would come from Lydia and the *Pure Gold* folks to hunt down me and Ben, who likely broke loose of the country club crowd easily enough. It's only a matter of time until the law or one of the brothers find me and it won't be in this damn car. It had caused way too much pain and destruction. But now the trouble was getting back up to the gorge. The club access road is the easiest but wouldn't be safe to go near until well after dark, that's far past too late. The only other way up was on the much more rugged logging road on the side facing the preserve. Beggars can't be choosers, though. As long as Cliff and Tammy were safe, I'd at least try to climb that mountain with whatever power this beat-up piece of shit had left.

So, once again, squinting my eyes and squeezing the steering wheel like a getaway driver, I slammed the gas hard and the car shot forward. It went about forty yards before it sputtered a little and then another twenty before it gave off coughing chugs and finally let out the familiar mechanical death rattle that whispered, "We're out of gas, motherfucker."

The gas gauge was busted like the rest of the car and, of course, it could've been a fuse, a malfunctioning line, or perhaps the devil settling into the job of taking over my life, but my layman's diagnosis was that this ride would go nowhere until I scared up some petrol. For a second, I scanned the neighboring homes with vehicles parked out front and imagined siphoning enough to get me up the mountain, until the reality of no can or hose or any prior experience with the process of sucking gas out of a tank sealed my fate. I snapped open the storage box near my elbow and hauled out an old pair of sunglasses. After donning the shades while climbing out of the truck and then thrusting hands deep into coat pockets and hanging head low, I broke into the five-minute hustle to Sully's gas station.

Luckily, Sully's is at the opposite end of town from the bypass connection, so unless someone randomly pulls off to grab a sandwich or ask directions, most folks motoring past Rock Hollow aren't even aware a filling station exists. As for the business itself, Tom Sullivan, whose family has owned the place forever, makes his profit from the appetites of humans rather than their vehicles. Without fail, the expansive refrigerated rows of beer and soda lining the walls, racks boasting candy, chips, and jerky, in addition to copious cigarettes and chewing tobacco on the shelves behind the register, are regularly dispensed faster than Tom can beg his suppliers to shuttle up to him. During those dry occasions, Tom hitches his trailer and drives to Portland to pick up temporary supplies, so he can get his store stocked up by sunrise to fulfill his client's desires for trans-fat, corn syrup, and suds, ensuring that gentleman Tom, the scion of Sully's, is destined to retire a rich man.

Approaching slowly up Hickory Street, where the gas station shares a corner along with Main, there were two folks and a dog in one home's front yard, and some young teen's wiffle ball game taking place in the back of another. Otherwise only a couple of cars, and no dangerous pickups, passed without incident so I took a deep breath and headed across Main Street.

Pushing open the door to the convenience store, which is attached to the pump island by a roof hardly big enough to protect customers from the elements, the cramped interior gave me the impression that either I had grown or it had shrunk since my last visit.

Logically, on a Sunday, Tom Sullivan was nowhere to be

found, and a skinny, blonde-headed kid stood up from a stool he had been planted on behind the register. His eyes were a weird shade of blue, and his long blonde hair was swept back behind his head in a mane. A slight smirk hung on his lips but he was friendly enough.

"Hello, sir," he chirped. "Gas or beer?"

"Uh, gas." I put my hands down on the counter and stared into those tiny, strange pools of blue. "Listen, I ran out just a few blocks away…"

"I'm sorry."

"That's life, right? So, I need a gas can full of unleaded."

"OK." he took a small step back and reached for a clipboard on a shelf. "I'll just need a driver's license. Huh, looks like the staties are in town."

He gestured over my shoulder, and I glanced back only slightly, expecting the cruiser to be sitting outside the door and the officers on their way inside to apprehend me, but the tail end of it moved down the road and out of sight.

Noticing for the first time the warm and stale air inside the store, I wiped the sweat from my cheeks and turned back to the kid.

"What do you need?"

"You got to leave your driver's license to get the gas can," he replied, nodding along with the regulation.

"Shoot. My ID's back in the car." My wallet was in the storage box of my truck, as if half a lie was an improvement on my part. "But, Son, I'm the sheriff of this town."

"I mean," he gestured to his forehead, "It says so on your hat. But you can buy anythin' online. One time, my mom bought a—"

"Kid, I'm really the sheriff. You can trust me."

"Oh, no. Sorry. You see, Mr. Sullivan got real mad when I let somebody take a can last month. They never came back, and even though he said he wouldn't deduct it out of my salary, I think he still—"

"Hold up," I said loudly, "I know Tom Sullivan. My kid does

his landscaping. So just give me the can, ring up three gallons of the cheap stuff."

Suddenly he looked as if he were going to throw up. "Uh, sorry, but I don't know you and…even if you are the sheriff, I really need this job. We just moved here—"

"You're about my son's age," I cut in warmly, although my hands were curling into strangulation mode. "Do you go to the high school in Marbleton?"

"Not yet. We got here around Christmas, and my mom was way late in gettin' me signed up, so they said she gotta homeschool me, and she's pissed about it, so that's not goin' so good. And then she said I gotta get out of the house more, so she made me get this job. But if you ask me—"

"OK. All right," I interrupted, not kindly. "I appreciate your family history, but all I need is you to give me a gas can."

"I'm sorry. Really, I am but like I said, the last time I gave one out, the guy never came back. And he was a real nice dude, too. Said he—"

"Just shut the fuck up." My words struck him with such force that he dropped the clipboard. "I'm not a customer anymore. I'm robbing the place."

"What?"

I lifted my coat. "See? Here's my gun. I don't know if they still say it on the cop shows anymore, but this is a stick-up. Get the can and fill it with unleaded."

"Geez!"

To his credit, the scared young man opened a cabinet, grabbed a can, banged a couple of keys on the register, and dashed out to get my fuel. As I waited outside by the door, he was a bit awkward opening the twist-top funnel, shaky hands and all, but he had it filled and capped in no time.

After he'd set it down near my feet, I led him back inside.

"Now get in the bathroom," I ordered and grabbed a couple of Hershey bars off a nearby shelf. "You got a cell phone?"

"Y-yes."

The tiny bathroom was nothing but a small closet with a toilet and sink and the kid sat down on the john.

"OK. After you shut that door, I want you to count to sixty and then call up the state police and tell them there's a robbery in progress."

"I don't know their number."

"Figure it out, son. And you tell them the man that robbed you is named Ben Hinckle, and I'm the same guy that shot up the Maple Syrup Festival. You got it? Ben Hinckle. Me and my brothers are driving a big red pickup with Jersey plates."

"I thought you was the sheriff?"

"It's just a fucking hat," I barked at him. "Now you finished asking questions?"

"Y-eah," he stammered while his body began shaking all over.

"It's a minor crisis, kid. Be a man and step up! Ben Hinckle, red pick-up, Jersey plates. Sixty seconds, starting now!"

I slammed the door to the bathroom and was about to take off when the shelves of cigarettes caught my eye. Leaning over the register, I grabbed a pack of Marlboro Reds, always the sharpest nails for your coffin, and a lighter with the words *Smoke Em Up* on it. In one swift motion, I ripped the pack open and lit one like the stolen lighter commanded.

My words came out mingled with the blue smoke like a devil's sigh. "Suppose this is who I am now."

I hurried out of the store, lugging the three-gallon red-plastic can, which felt like fifty pounds to my abused body. Yet, along with a pretty good tasting cigarette, I managed to jam down one and a half candy bars while I jogged-walked, getting to within sight of the car before the sirens sounded, delivering solace that the cruiser would be busy for a precious few minutes while I gassed my ride up.

Every single blessed moment of this day had involved stumbling over one hurdle after another, so I wasn't surprised by the middle-aged man in running shorts, a teal tank-top and slippers sitting near the car on a beach chair at the edge of his scraggly lawn. He appeared harmless enough, reading the newspaper and drinking a can of beer, so I hustled down the sidewalk with my arm and shoulder going numb from the weight of what now felt like a two-ton gas can.

"This your car?" he asked in a surprised manner.

"Yup, ran out of gas," I replied with a wide grin, jostling the fuel cap off and hoisting the can's funnel into the tank.

"Ain't you the sheriff?"

"Right again!" I got the gas pouring and then sized up the man. "Are you the neighborhood watch?"

"Nah. I'm just catchin' some rays."

"Good luck with that," I chuckled with a nod skyward.

An awkward silence took over as the gas glugged and the man checked me out with side-eye glances.

"You know they say April sun is the best thing for a body. Better than July."

"Sort of nippy out, though."

"You gotta build up a tolerance. Like spring trainin' for a suntan."

"Well, this is wind-burn weather." I suggested while twisting the cap back on and slapping the fuel door shut. "Anyway, friend. I gotta go."

"That car is messed up," he offered as a farewell.

We both turned towards the direction of the sirens, now growing louder, as the staties were pulling out of the gas station. The search was on for the man named Ben Hinckle who'd told the dim-witted attendant that he was sheriff and then stole three gallons of gas, two Hershey bars, a pack of butts and a lighter.

"That's three brilliant statements you've made in a row," I announced with feigned glee. "Guess what? You win a gas can! Here, catch."

I tossed the can over the car and the man watched it land on the sidewalk. He looked at me as if his understanding of local law enforcement was in flux.

"Do a couple of minutes of community service and bring it

back to Sulley's, OK? God bless America."

I gave a big salute as I got in the car, and he slowly returned one of his own. Giving two toots of the horn while pulling away, I saw in the side mirror that he was picking up the can, another heartening sign there are still good folks out there and a sickening reminder how much my family was fucking up the normalcy of this town. *Well, they ain't seen nothin' yet.* There was little chance that my job could survive this train-wreck weekend and knowing the two candidates that ran against me in the last election— a young drunk and an old pervert— the populace of Rock Hollow had better be ready for some unstable times.

While I retraced the path through the neighborhoods that Cliff and I had taken earlier away from the mountain, the chocolate bars in my belly were doing the opposite of their intended purpose, and my knotted stomach began offering juicy belches, even as my mouth went dry. I was pretty sure the products of the Hershey company would not stay in my stomach for much longer.

After pulling over and pushing the door open, I slid my body down onto the seat and hung my head outside but the heaving that followed offered nothing but a few dark lines of spit, and I figured that the candy was not to blame. Because the needle that gauges my usually rock-steady nervous system had finally pushed way deep into the danger zone, it actually felt so good for the moment to just lower my head down and stare at the cracked asphalt while the sirens wailed even further off, signifying the staties heading for the other side of town. Good thinking, fellas. The clear path to a successful getaway lay in the bypass, then the interstate and onward to wherever.

So tempting was the prospect of cashing in my chips and taking to the highway, riding as far as I could and then ditching the car to hitchhike for another long, long way. Yet, a stinging guilt about my treatment of the poor kid at the gas station clouded my image of flight. So, I'm pulling guns on teenagers now? What the fuck? But what was really giving me the creeps was the huge shadow of Keith Griffin, because he still seemed more alive than dead, continuing to be a scourge in this town and probably fucking with me even further now that he'd got a hold of a bag of tricks in the afterlife.

In the strangest way, lying here with my head hanging out of the car was the most relaxed I'd felt in days. Although my body badly needed a bowling ball sized ibuprofen and about a week's worth of sleep, my mind was slowly unwinding everything that had happened over the last forty-eight hours while the soft plush seating and some steady breathing released pressure from my pounding head. The coughs and unsteady rumble of the idling engine began to take on a strange rhythm. It felt wonderful to close my eyes and even laugh a little while thinking about Keith with a big goblet of the Lord's wine, cussing out the angels and taking the first flight back to our world to kick everybody's ass. Probably, he'd start with the ones that owed him money, but for certain he'd be targeting his black magic on his old buddy Blake. *Come and get me, Keith, but I gotta warn you I don't have too much left. Dirty business, life and death. Such a dirty business. Man, oh, man…Oh, man…*

"Wake up, sleepin' beauty!'

The stink of exhaust and the darker shade of asphalt gave me a weird, dreamlike impression that I had crawled up inside the motor like a squirrel and I was warm and snoozing in the belly of the machine. Jerking my eyes open from the doze, I found I was lying halfway out of the car in the shadow of something big. When I looked up, the closest thing to my head was the barrel of a shotgun. At the other end of the gun was Dicky's ugly face hanging out of the pickup, which had pulled up tight to the car, its bumper almost touching my open door.

In my wrecked and sleepy state, Dicky's face looked like Keith Griffin's, and Derrick's booming laugh from the driver's seat of the truck added a satanic quality to the waking nightmare. For a brief moment, it felt like I had finally made it to hell. An overpowering rush of loss and fear convulsed my body as I jerked fully to my senses, bringing my head back to thump hard on the door frame. Only instincts culled from so much time out on the road launched my hand up wildly toward the gearshift in a sudden urge to get the out of there fast. Within a half-second of my hand touching the shift and dropping it into reverse; I pushed my foot down hard on the gas pedal.

If I hadn't pulled my other arm inside, it likely would have been ripped off along with the car door, which whined terribly and then vanished in a crunch as I scraped backwards along the side of the truck. The squeal of metal on metal couldn't entirely cover Dicky's hollering and cussing, the two sounds mingling into discordant getaway music. Or at least *attempted* getaway, as I wasn't going anywhere fast. Fortunately, the car only hooked onto the truck's fender for a moment and then gave way, so I spun it around and just barely missed a telephone pole on the opposite sidewalk.

Derrick started pulling around to block the street, so after steamrolling right at him, I swerved onto the sidewalk to plow across a gateless front yard and then through the small unpainted picket fence of the house next door. After spinning out on the brown grass and mud while struggling to get the seat belt secured, I got back onto the road. Certainly, driving without a door proved surprisingly difficult, although the blasting cold air knocked the sleep right out of me.

Back at the near-ambush site, the brothers were having difficulty turning the truck around to follow. I had apparently knocked a parked car into the street after my shortcut through the yards. My hunk of junk would never reach the speed to outrun them, even though it let me push it up to seventy-five after taking the first wild turn. The engine was knocking and gray-black smoke was flying out of the muffler like an old, spiraling WWI plane strafed by one too many hits from the Red Baron. I put a hand to my temple as it now felt like wearing a headache-helmet.

Shit. I could hear the truck catching up fast, and there was no chance I'd get to the mountain, let alone the gorge. Just as I was accepting the fact that the brothers would probably settle for nothing less than a gunfight, I rode up on a familiar muddy patch of tractor tires along the side of the road and at once slammed on the brakes.

The town dump! There's nobody there on Sunday, not even Carl Deavers, the keeper of the place, who would be in town, drunk out of his mind playing Keano at *The Deuce*. Recently, Carl and I had come to loggerheads over his digging of a new landfill, which he had widened to three times the legal length, dangerously bordering the access road, and so deep that he thought he'd struck oil, but it ended up being just sludge.

I whipped the car around and pulled onto the gravelly dirt road just as the brothers roared up and slammed on their own brakes. There was no time for another plan, and the only way to shake these guys was to put them out of action. Despite my desire to try to save a shred of my soul by never killing anyone again, I was going to do something dangerous, maybe fatal. Without pausing to consider the risk, I hurtled my doorless ride straight toward Carl's new garbage pit.

The long dump road was a straight shot through packed mud and potholes the size of kiddy pools before reaching the burn pits and landfills. While avoiding the craters of water, I also had to tear around massive heaps of trash on both sides that Carl had been saving for a big grand opening dump, trying hard to elude the brothers without actually losing them before my trap could be sprung. After the third zigzag around the piles of trash and debris, I slid back onto the road and made straight for the hole. The car was shaking, and for a moment I thought it would seize up completely, but when I floored the accelerator, it delivered a nice jump that stretched the gap between the car and their truck by twenty yards.

That's when I swerved hard around a big corner near the foot of the new, oversized landfill and jammed the brakes, throwing the vehicle into a complete 360. In these dizzying moments, my eyes shut tight, breath coming fast until the car came to a rest. The seconds ticked as I waited for the brothers to master the same turn and smash straight into me. Instead, the desperate plan somehow worked as the truck whizzed past not three feet in front of my car and launched into the air above the empty landfill, a screaming mass of red aluminum, black-rubber tires spinning wildly in the open space until the front body tilted forward and it dropped straight down, crashing into the rocky dirt floor in an ugly cacophony of broken glass, crunching steel and splintering plastic.

I sat watching the wreck below for any sign of occupants crawling out with guns blazing, but the prospects were doubtful. After nose-diving, the truck had landed upside down in the dirt and mud and was a smashed-up mess. The entire dump had fallen into a strange quiet except for the pickup's engine ticking in a death rattle and the rear wheels still spinning in a futile search for hard ground.

Seconds closed in on a full minute and still nobody climbed out. No smoke was coming from the engine block, which I took to mean that fire or explosion wasn't likely, making me wonder if I should hang around. The sons-of-bitches would throw a match on my ride if I were in the same shape, so screw them, right? Right? *Ah, damn it!*

I jammed the car into park and got out, growling against the ever-present full-body pain, also scolding myself about precious gas wasted because I didn't dare turn the engine off for fear it wouldn't ever start again. Risking everything to check on the safety of two scumbags, I moved around the pit to the path on the other side where Carl had left a wide inclined slope of dirt to get his big excavator in and out. The dirt was slick from melted snow, and I had to slide half-way down, rubbing away the burning in my hip as I reached the floor of the landfill. The truck's front windshield was a dense mass of jagged spiderweb cracks and missing glass, which made me wonder if the fall might've killed them both. A flush of momentary sadistic glee jackknifed right into guilt.

"Hey in there!" I shouted while slowing my approach.

"Help…" Dicky groaned from inside the half-crushed cab.

"Can you get out?" I bent down and peered into the destroyed passenger-side window that was compacted to half its size.

If it had been a cloudy day, I wouldn't be alive to tell the tale because the sun caught the muzzle of the shotgun a whisker of a second before it exploded and the harsh scream of a slug zipped past my head. I fell backward into a roll, nostrils full of carbon from the near-fatal miss and then scrambled to reach the window. When the rifle protruded from the cab again, I yanked it hard and out of Dicky's hands, then used the butt of it to slam around inside a bunch of times, catching him at least twice, judging by the howls of pain.

"You son-of-a-bitch!" I hollered, "I was trying to help you!"

"Fuck you!" Dicky screamed.

Dropping down on my knees and peering in carefully through the crunched and smashed back window, I could see that Dicky was hanging upside down, clipped in by his seatbelt, but Derrick apparently didn't believe in buckling up and was lying in a heap on the inside of the roof.

"You gotta get out of there. Truck might catch fire."

"Seatbelts stuck. Help me," Dicky pleaded, and the tone was so much like the first time that it struck me as suspicious.

Taking a leather work glove out of my jacket pocket, I stuck it over the butt end of the rifle. While pressing back against the wrecked body of the truck, I began slowly reaching it toward the window. This time the gunshot hit squarely in the center of the glove and knocked the rifle out of my hand. Who knows how many weapons they've got stocked up in there?

I began making tracks for the muddy ramp, calling over my shoulder, "I ain't ever tried to help somebody that's shooting at me. So good luck getting out yourself!"

"You motherfucker!" Dicky suddenly found renewed energy. "I'll kill you."

He popped another couple of shots off, but I was careful not to cross his line of fire. Once I'd reached the top of the hole, he simply went on raging curses my way while I got into the car, turned it around and resumed the rudely interrupted passage to the gorge. That's when the damn little voice popped up again. If the dump road had been maybe a quarter-mile shorter, I would have already been safely cruising up the mountain to roll the car off the edge and get reunited with my family, but that piece of absolute shit called my conscience began chirping away. What if the two of them were dying back there, unable to get out? That heap could ignite easily, burning both brothers alive.

I stopped at the dump entrance and looked at the clear, empty road leading up to the mountain. With no further hesitation, I gave into whatever stupid fucking goodness was left in me and turned toward town.

Maybe as a sign of instant karma but more likely just due to the man's plain laziness, my friend in the lawn chair was still out enjoying a beer and soaking up the weak early spring rays when I clattered back into his neighborhood. He almost tipped backwards when I screeched up on the opposite sidewalk across from him.

"Hey!" I shouted as he regained his balance and stood up.

"I tol' you I'd take that can back. You don't gotta check up on me. Shit, man, now you got no door!"

"Call up the hospital in Marbleton. Understand? Marbleton General," I was short of breath, and my nerves were jumping. "Say it's an emergency and tell 'em to get an ambulance out to the Rock Hollow dump."

"What for?" He had lost his shock and began crossing the street.

"Big wreck," My voice cracked, and I coughed hard. "Somebody might be dying."

"Shit," he said as he arrived at the car and looked at me with well-deserved caution.

I reached out and grabbed the beer from his hand and sucked the last of it down, handing him back the empty can.

"Somebody's gonna die. Hurry!"

The man turned and made off for his house, pulling out a cell phone from his pocket. Not enough people like that screwball in the world, for sure. When I took off, I could see him by his front steps blabbering to somebody on the other line, likely first calling for the ambulance to get to the dump and then probably scheduling the white wagon to come and take the town's sheriff to the funny farm.

Whipping the car around and out of this now familiar neighborhood, I sort of wished that I'd confiscated that guy's beer cooler to get some liquid medication in my blood, anything to soothe my cranky joints and muscles. Instead, I had the chilling wind whipping all over my body, keeping me focused on the road. Somehow, I even found the energy to scream a loud "fuck you to hell!" as I passed the dump. The curse wasn't necessarily meant for the brothers, even though they deserved a damning more than anyone outside of my family for the trouble they've caused, but more of a resistance to any thought of surrender, even after all the awful events piled one on top of the other in the past two days. I had to get it done right now because it'd become clear that I had reached what folks call the "dead end of one's wits." The obvious result of hammering straight into one brick wall of punishment after another, each has taken its toll, and even just one more might be the end of me.

The throbbing pulse of pain in my head grew worse as I had to shake it violently every minute to stop my eyes from closing and keep the car in the right lane. A few cars passed on their way down the mountain, probably some festival goers who arrived late and turned back at the sight of the parking logjam. I didn't want to look their way in case one might be Ben, even though his big red truck was a heap of junk and the ceremonial first deposit in Carl Deaver's landfill. You couldn't put carjacking past him at this point, so I made a cursory glance at the last vehicle that passed and got three innocently stunned faces of a man and two women in return, staring dumbfounded at my doorless, sputtering, smoking near-wreck of a ride.

As I neared the logging road, my head ticked off the miles and the scarcity of gas left before reaching the top of the mountain. The fun really began once I turned onto the bumpy old, forgotten passage leading up and over the mountain, mostly touched by foot traffic in the decades since horse-drawn wagons fell to the automobile. The few recreational four-wheelers and snowmobiles that cut along this wide path had kept it clear of impassable foliage, but the ride up was far worse than the one Cliff and I had taken on our escape from the country club.

Every red light and warning sensor on the dashboard was lit or blinking incessantly as I pushed the car upward, revving it hard through stuck wheels and nearly being impaled by the end of a cracked tree limb that flew in through the open door, one branch taking a slice of my forearm with it. Watching the blood pool on my skin, I couldn't help but think that this whole mess was intended to punish nobody else but me. Not the town, not my family, just me. "Born under a bad sign" is the saying, and if you look at all the shit that's happened to us, I was the only one bleeding all over himself and busted up and torn apart. Not Cliff, not Tammy. The Hinckle brothers deserved every knock in the head they got, but not their sister and not…

That poor kid. That's who I was bleeding and suffering for. The boy named Philly.

Just as my thoughts turned darker, the blue sky opened up above the trees on the mountaintop ahead. I hit the gas to make one last buzz-saw push to the crest, but as hard as the lurches and bumps shook me, the kid was all I could think about. His name was Phillip, hence the moniker of Philly, a cool nickname like a pool shark known only as Tex or a running back called Hollywood.

As much shit as Cliff had coming to him, damn it, at least he was alive. Without knowing Philly at all except for the last sight of his dead body at the creek side, all kinds of images of what he might've done and who he could've become ran wild in my head. Was he a member of one of the gangs that rode trail-bikes at the Preserve, leaving beer cans and used condoms wherever they camped? Or was he a smart kid, spending his weekends with his face stuffed in books and his mother begging him to go out and throw a ball around. Maybe he would've gone on to college and got out of this town like we wanted for Cliff. That final thought struck deeply along with the bitter end to any hope that I had for my own boy to have some kind of future. Perhaps I could've saved him just by being a better man and husband and father.

Finally, something inside me snapped and broke the dam that had held for so long. I started crying, screaming at the top of my lungs in the empty woods, damning this life for all its evil and far too little good. Even the sight of the flattening terrain and sky now clearly visible through the trunks of pines crowded upon the mountaintop did nothing to calm my nerves. My entire body clenched—tight chest, wrenched gut, aching arms, stiffened legs, squeezing the last burst of energy out as I punched the dash hard until my hand bled.

With the last vapors of fuel in the tank, I pushed the car out of the wood line to a sliding stop on the stony edge of the gorge.

The view from up there, as has been discovered by hikers and campers ignoring posted signs directing them otherwise, is simply staggering and quickly shook me out of the opening salvo of a nervous breakdown. Although my chest still heaved with sobs, I managed to wipe my eyes dry and gaze across the miles upon miles of treetops rolling on in the distance. Aside from the fir trees, most were still bare of leaves awaiting the warm days of May to sprout. Still, it looked like an ocean of brown and green. Then my glance slid toward the stunning creation of nature that is the gorge.

Past the cliff's edge which dropped off precipitously about ten feet ahead of the car, its dark gray and black walls stretched out and downward like the gaping throat of some kind of giant entity, yawning wide like an enormous leviathan, welcoming all it could swallow.

After such a long, hard journey to get here, I was unable to move. The moment was too achingly peaceful, with nobody around and all the travails of life way back down the mountain. Everybody in town was going along with their Sunday routine…except for Philly.

The stark image of that kid on the roadside pulsed back into my head, causing all the sheer and immense beauty around me to collapse. What only moments ago had seemed like a corner of heaven turned into yet another scene of punishment. My leg, which had been pressing hard on the brake, cramped and as I eased it slightly, the car lurched forward. Still six feet of space in front of me, but now the drop-off was even more visible. From the very edge, one couldn't see the bottom. Many partygoers' beer bottles had been tossed over to test the height of its drop but always splashed so far down below that the litterbug could barely hear it. That's where this car was going, into the dead silence of a deep run of water, down there where time would be the only one to find it. God did that sound like a nice ending. Jesus, it *looked* so nice.

The walls of the gorge were streaked with long, bright lines, probably where the pressure of gravity had done its business and a similar crushing force steadily did its work on me, almost as if it was opening up as both a solution and escape. Floating into my thoughts was a weird memory of childhood, back when I was crazy about vampires, always so taken by their ability to capture prey in a trance and then sucking the life out of them. I tried to get Cliff hooked on them, too but he said he liked Frankenstein's monster better because you can't kill him. Instead, he just disappears in a big blaze and you never see him again. Problem solved…until the next time.

Problem solved, disappear in a big blaze, until the next time. Shit. No. What next time? But…maybe…yes. What did they actually have to pin on Cliff and Tammy if I rode this car down to the bottom of the gorge? Nothing, if they kept their mouths shut. Tammy was smart enough to figure it out. She could say I did it. I hit the kid.

Holy mother, it's like the solution was waiting for me up here, and it took a long battle and journey to figure it out. I just wished I could say goodbye. My heart felt so heavy in my chest. To give my family any chance at happiness, I had to leave them. I suppose I always knew that was the answer, but I thought it meant taking off to another place and never contacting them again. But I guess this was sort of similar except I wouldn't be so fucking tired. I was beat. Totally beat.

Easing up even more on the brake caused the car to slide further than I had planned, leaving barely a foot between the front tires and the edge, maybe less. My knee was burning, and I told myself that there'd be no more pain in another few seconds, a sadly welcoming thought. Enough damage had been done; this was a sort of redemption, and anything that cleanses the soul through fire takes bravery. I eased slightly up, and now the front wheels were at the edge. Some rocks started giving way, and ever so slightly, the car slid forward.

Out of nowhere, a small, almost cartoon rendition of the first notes of *The Twilight Zone* theme song began playing lightly. I was aghast that, after all the punishment the universe had laid on me, it'd finish me off to the strains of such an idiotically performed soundtrack. Then the tune was matched with the image in my head of Cliff's smiling face. He was so proud the day that he'd gotten his first cell phone, and he'd paid me a compliment by using a ringtone that cracked me up. That's it! Cliff's phone was somewhere in the car.

I turned to look at the back seat, and the vehicle gave another slight slide forward. Carefully, I clicked the seat belt lock. As I eased it off, it seemed almost like the ringtone was underneath me, so I slowly placed my hand between the seat and fished the phone out. Louder than ever, the song chirped. I closed my eyes and took a deep breath before answering it.

"Hello." I could hardly manage a whisper.

"Blake," Tammy shrieked across the line, "Where are you?"

"Listen, honey, is Cliff there?"

"Yes, we're at the safe place. Come here now." Her pleading was so emotional that it pained me to hear it.

I fought hard to speak. The edge was very close, and the walls of the gorge were doing the vampire trance-thing. *Come here, my child, come here.*

"No, I'm going down with the car into the gorge. You're gonna say I killed little Philly, and I couldn't live with it anymore."

"No, Blake!!" she screamed. "Don't! I—"

"You'll be safe. I love you guys," I blubbered, resigning to let go of everything. "I'm going now…I…"

"Stop!!" Tammy almost came through the phone with her wail. "I did it! I did it!! I killed that boy! God, stop Blake, please! Stop!"

"You?"

"It was Keith's idea to…he said…you'd kill us if you found out! And then…oh Jesus! Cliff tried to save me! He didn't do it! I did!"

"You…" I whimpered.

"Please don't do it! Blake, that poor boy's dead," she cried, "but we're alive! You and me and Cliff. We're alive!"

It was too late. The loose rocks under the front tires crumbled, and then the soil fell away, and the car pitched forward.

If the door hadn't been ripped off earlier, I would've sailed over to an ugly end.

With the last trail of a moment to spare, I rolled out and landed on the hard stone. I shut my eyes tight until the distant crashes of the car bouncing off jagged walls rang from below, followed by a small explosion, then the final splash of the wreck plunging into deep water cut off all the ugly racket. Some folks on the mountain had probably heard the commotion, but I didn't care. I don't know anybody who's ever risked the treacherous climb down into the gorge and it seemed a safe bet that no one would try it anytime soon.

"Blake! Blake!" Tammy's little voice implored. I'd forgotten that the phone was still clutched in my hand.

"Hey, honey," I croaked and rolled over onto my back, staring up at the deep blue afternoon sky. My vision was all fucked up. "Stay put. I'll get there soon. I just found a parking spot."

She said something in reply, but who knows if it was praise or damnation? I caught one last look at a small, thin trail of exhaust smoke easing its way to disbursement in the air, the last evidence from the cursed, mangled machine, now out of sight but never out of mind. When my eyes fell shut again, they stayed that way for a long while.

Chapter Ten

Unintentionally waking up on the ground is something to be avoided in life. Just one walk through any furniture store will exhibit the human desire for soft, feathery beds, held steadfastly by frames of solid wood or metal and lavish upholstery. These items are tucked in the bedrooms of every home across the land as icons to humanity's evolution from apes snoozing in the treetops to modern men and women knocking out eight hours of cozy slumber. Even the rugged outdoors enthusiasts of modern times savor the returns of lugging around an extra fifteen pounds of air mattress and hand-pump in a backpack to lie comatose and content under the stars, while their less prepared companions toss and turn on a spongy cut of foam that offers no more protection from hard ground than an oversized yoga mat. The earth's surface is to be trod, dug up, bought and sold, but not directly slept upon—merely common sense by this point in human history, unless, that is, you're as busted up as I was, then any old patch of dirt will do.

When I first blinked my eyes open, the ground beneath me, with its gritty dirt, tufts of weeds, and earthy smell, had never felt sweeter to my shocked yet grateful senses. I lifted my head and took a full, startled body roll away from the edge of the rocky cliff, catching just a glimpse of the cavernous drop. I had been lying less than a foot away from it. One sleepy turn to the wrong side and I would've fallen to my death. It still felt so close, the end of life, it hurt terribly.

Matching my pained spirit were the body aches staging a strong comeback in thick waves. I tried to get up, and my back, shoulders and knees lit on fire. My throat was bone dry, and I thought about looking for a bottle of water in the car before recalling that the vehicle was now slumbering with the fish. So, after rolling about like a bug for a few seconds, I was able to sit up and recall the parade of shit that had led me here.

The car. The car was gone. Right. It had to be done because…Oh my Lord, Tammy. Tammy did it. Now, instead of Cliff, she'd have to stand up and take what's coming. And had she said something about Keith? What ugly shit had been going on behind my back that led to her killing a boy?

I felt a bitter satisfaction rising, the devil inside of me saying that they both got what they deserved, but the truth is that I loved Tammy and any punishment she took would also rip a piece out of me. We're the same person in a bunch of ways. So, if she has to go down hard, there was no reason to make it open and shut. I'm still glad I got rid of the car, that fucking smoking gun. Let the legal machinery do its thing to her in slow motion, so she could adapt to the inevitable endgame. We were trying to get Cliff through this mess in one piece, and now I've got to find a way to help her, too. Don't I?

I mean, the mere mention of Keith Griffin. Damn her to…Woah! Back up! Cliff was free, sort of. He'd certainly get hit with some kind of accessory charge but a good lawyer would knock that down. They'd also nail me to the wall, but fuck them, go ahead, all I did was marry the wrong gal. Shit, maybe they'd figure the worst punishment for us both was to force Tammy and I to share a cell.

The sun was steadily making its way to it's resting place in the West, apparently my little nap had been only about twenty minutes, but to my head it had given the effect of a whole night's slumber. I still ached all over, but at least I had some clarity. To my surprise there wasn't the least urge to fulfill the duty of the sheriff's office. The guilt that had previously driven me to uphold the law and protect the innocent was all gone, replaced with a suffocating malaise of failure. The awful shame of the cuckolded husband followed the sharp cuts of guilt and inadequacy in swift succession.

Added to my being a shitty father and it summed me up as an overall miserable human being. All my life, everything I'd ever learned, loved, or accomplished had brought nothing but tragedy and confusion to those around me. Fuck being a good man; it just was not cut out for me. I should've robbed banks. At least that would've given me a choice between taking a life or not. There was no human choice in this one. That kid, Philly, had no say in how he went, and I hope he's up there in heaven. Maybe Tammy had no choice, either. I'd constantly ignored her, and for the longest time whenever we're together we ended up fighting like enemies, so maybe the only way she could stay sane with a man like me was by sleeping with somebody worse. No fair, no foul. She was following a terrible path that we had laid down together, but it appeared we were finally arriving at the end of it.

"Oh…Oh, God!"

Standing was difficult and walking proved almost impossible at first, muscles tight with dehydration and mouth sour with the aftertaste of beer and chocolate, dizziness, tongue swelling, basically half-alive. As I continued into the woods for the long walk to town, my legs warmed up and the trail got easier about halfway down, but everything, and I mean everything, looked and felt different. This no longer seemed the welcoming place it had been since my earliest years. The paths all looked barren and rough, the sky blotted out by slumping tree branches appearing as if they may never reach upward again.

I sulked through the entire walk, chewing hard on my failures, and when stopping to catch my breath not even the cold smack of creek water that I swallowed in desperate gulps and splashed on my face could shake me out of the funk. These woods had always been a part of my life, part of me really, and now the comforting familiarity had been blasted away, leaving a place in which I felt unwelcome; somewhere I didn't belong.

After a long while, I reached the main road again. The depression hardly lifted, but my mind set its machinery onto matters still in flux in the outside world. Hoping to catch a ride from someone coming down the mountain, I tried to wipe the dirt off my face and came away with a good deal of caked blood. I suppose it doesn't matter how dirty you are if you look like you got hit by a bus. A couple of drivers did not share the sentiment and raced right past me, ignoring my frantic waving for them to pull over. Hell, I didn't blame them. I sure didn't look like the Rock Hollow sheriff right now, and the basic job requirements of swagger and guts were buried under an avalanche of fatigue.

The five-mile hike back to the station would almost kill me but stopping there was imperative before heading to meet the family at the safe place, even if it took hours. The sound of an oncoming vehicle interrupted these desperate calculations. Before I could even turn to signal for them to stop, a Jeep pulled up alongside me with the smiling face of Toby Jeffers behind the wheel. Perfect timing. He must've been on the way back from birdwatching up the mountain.

"Sheriff," he said warmly as he rolled the passenger window down, his large, bespectacled Santa Claus face peeking out, "I thought it was you. Holy hell! You all right?"

"Yeh. I had a long day." I leaned hard against the passenger door. "Could use a ride, though."

"Well, why don't you just make like a frog and hop in!"

Toby was famous for such cringe-inducing jokes, and it often earned him time alone at *The Deuce* after his pals tired of hearing ancient trinkets of humor. Right now, the effect was music to my ears. The toasty warm interior of the Jeep matched with smooth classical music on the stereo, were a balm to my nerves. Before we set out, Toby handed over a bag of salted peanuts and a cold, dripping can of ginger ale from his cooler in the back seat, giving me a surprisingly nice airplane-ride vibe.

"Now what in the hell have you been up to?" he bellowed after handing me the refreshments.

I didn't respond right away. Toby gave me a long glance and then got the Jeep going, taking some big gulps from his own can of ginger ale, followed by careful belches into his hand as he drove.

"Well," I began after a mouthful of salty peanuts and a sip of soda, "I haven't really had any sleep since Friday night…"

For the rest of the ride, I detailed the events of the last couple of days and nights omitting the incriminating parts. A lawyer can try to wrestle those out of me later. We even shared a good laugh at the idea of Lydia Bernard becoming the target for Tammy's pudding-tossing performance. Toby listened attentively to the entire tale culminating in the fib at how my car had broken down while trying to beat country club traffic by taking the logging road, and on the way out that I'd tumbled down a slippery embankment and got cut up in the woods.

When I finally finished, he was so excited that he launched into recounting the blow-by-blow adventure of his bird-spotting expedition, these being red-letter days of arrival after migration for certain types in the region. Toby is part of a small online bunch of enthusiasts who, outside of jobs and families, spend any spare time in the early spring braving the chilly temperatures and muddy terrain to capture the most "first-time eyes" on feathered friends. After getting decent images on his phone of a Snow goose and an Eastern Phoebe, he was going to be cock of the walk in the next group meeting.

The town looked fairly normal as we cruised down Main Street. Folks were outside of the diner trading stories, and a couple of smokers lingered on the sidewalk in front of *The Deuce*, while a dog walker or two passed. All pleasant late Sunday afternoon stuff. The best sight of all was my truck parked outside of the station. Tammy, in her special way, had been fatally stupid in her dealings with this whole big mess and yet had proven a sharp cookie by figuring that I'd return here and find my ride. Toby was happy to honor my request to be dropped at the back of the building, although from what I could see everything seemed to check out, with no state police cruiser in sight. Hopefully, they were out rounding up Ben Hinckle. The coast seemed clear enough, so I got ready to exit the Jeep in my unintentional imitation of an elderly man suffering from chronic everything.

"You're a good man, Toby," I groaned during the slow climb out. "I hope you win your bird contest."

"Oh, don't worry," he beamed, "I'm gonna kick ass!"

We traded pleasantries, and he drove away. It might have been the peanuts or the ginger ale or probably just the good nature of Toby, but calm had settled upon me. Maybe Toby had shown me that I needed to spend the rest of my days out in the woods spotting birds making their way back from vacation. The idea of spending long hours seeking little pea-brained balls of feathers sounded pretty damn welcoming right about now.

Due to Barbara's rushed departure earlier, the back door was unlocked, and I opened it quietly. Stacey wasn't due to arrive for another hour and you can bet Barbara called to warn her to stay away after everything went down, particularly the piece-of-shit Hinckle brothers messing with her family. I expected to find at least ten messages on my cell phone asking for the night off. That's OK, I needed one myself.

The back room was dark, but also familiar and I quickly and quietly navigated around the crates of junk ranging from Christmas decorations to old road hazard signs and stacks of grimy orange cones, as well as the crates of old files that the state requires us to keep. I'd almost reached the door when I bumped into a badly piled stack of boxes, tipping the top one over. The papers it held spilled noisily onto the floor.

"Shit," I whispered and fumbled for the doorknob.

"Hello?" a man's voice called from inside the station house.

My palm rested on the cold knob. There was certainly time to make a hasty escape, but who knew how much running I had left in my legs. No more fleeing like a rabbit. Take the fucking snare and let them cook you for dinner.

"Hello?" the same voice spoke even louder this time.

If it was state police, they'd have rushed through the door by now, and it wasn't Ben Hinckle's nasty rasp. Because I was so damn tired of fighting and retreating, I closed my hand tight and turned the knob to face the unknown, although my slightly recovering mental capabilities had it all worked out as the door swung open.

Waiting for me inside the station were the two hikers from Keith Griffin's place.

When I slowly moved into the office area, the young man took a step forward while holding his hands before him disarmingly. The woman was sitting in a chair by the door, and her face was full of concern, but nothing like the scared shitless look she'd worn the last time we met. They were both dressed up in the latest chic outerwear and didn't much look like the two scruffy hikers whose ass I'd saved. I shook my head at them for they were living proof that there is truly no escape from my many sins.

"Oh, gosh, hello, I…" the man stammered and ran a hand through his thick, amply gelled brown hair, "...we didn't mean to…We've been waiting for you."

"What do you want?" I stopped near the two small cells, gripping one of the bars for balance while my head swam.

He looked over at the woman, who seemed to urge him on silently. "We…know what you…you know, that man in the woods...."

"His name was Keith Griffin."

"We saw what you…" He averted his eyes. "What you did."

"So?" I looked from one to the other. "Huh? So?"

What kind of game were these two playing here? They get away from a crazy bastard in the wilderness and now they're back to blackmail the sheriff. For what? Their car was worth more than a year of my salary. They could try to take my soul, but that's bound for hell. Other than that, I had nothing.

"Listen…" I began with no clue what I was going to say next, but it didn't matter.

"We want to thank you," the woman piped in, standing quickly and moving next to her mate. "We know that crazy man could've…"

She was right to leave it dangling because there really was no telling what Keith might've done to them. She took her partner's arm and held it tight.

"We also have something to confess," Her voice quieted, and she looked me square in the eye. "We saw you bury him and well, we had to…We dug him back up."

"What in the hell for?" I let myself drop onto a stool by the jail cell.

"My phone," the man said with a pained face.

None of us said anything for moment, and then he continued.

"He must've had it on him when you…buried him. So, after we traced it back there, I…we dug him up."

"We didn't want any trouble," the woman interjected, "and we still don't. We just wanted the phone. So, nobody could trace it to us and ask about…"

Again, with the trailing words. It felt awful but I broke out laughing and, even though neither one of them joined in, I couldn't stop for about a minute. Everybody and their goddamn fucking phones.

"Well, where the hell is he now?" I asked wide-eyed after regaining some composure.

They looked at each other, finally coming to an agreement in their nervous silence. I liked the way they talked to each other without saying a word, sort of like Tammy and I used to be in the old days.

"In the river," the man blurted.

"You dragged his body all the way to the river?"

"No," She gestured the process with her hands. "First, we put him in his truck…"

"Took forever to find the keys," the man whispered, shamefully voicing a lingering annoyance.

"Then we drove him to the river," she continued, "and we dumped it, I mean, him, you know, the truck with him inside. And we sent that rifle down, too. So there's—"

"OK…" This time I cut her words off before they could dangle, even though I was stunned, not by the turn of events but that anything could surprise me at this point. "That brings us back to what I asked before. What do you want?"

She burst into quick emotional words, "To thank you. We're sorry. We didn't want trouble. Ever. I cried the whole time we dug that man up."

"She really did," the man nodded, with the slightest cringe.

"And really…we just want to go away and forget it ever happened, but we figured it's only right that…you should know."

I stared at them both for a few seconds and then stood and limped over to him. The man was about my height, and he stared at my chest while she looked away.

"Forget it," I offered. "That son-of-a-bitch had it coming to him from ten different directions. You two just got caught in the crossfire."

They both launched into profuse thanks and when I got them to stop, they also confirmed that the state police were none the wiser. They had told them they had lost their dog and wanted to report it to the sheriff's office.

By the time I walked them to the door, I had their sworn promise to hit the road and steer clear of this town in the future. Strangely, I had started to like them both. They carried an air of innocence that was kind of heartbreaking. The woman even gave me a small hug before they exited.

"Thank you for saving us. You're a good person."

"You know," the man offered in farewell advice, waving a finger at his own face, "you should, um, probably get iodine or something on those cuts. We like to use medical-grade honey."

After they left, I watched them through the window. They got in their car and drove off while my wasted nerves screamed for my mind to realize it all as a trick, but when they disappeared, my sense of caution eased up. I got on the phone and called Stacey to tell her to take as many nights off as she wanted, then said goodbye repeatedly due to all the frantic questions she fired at me. Next, I called Barbara to apologize for Ben's roughing up her husband and asked her to get rid of Keith Griffin's warrant. Barbara was a good egg and only had one question, although for certain she'd pepper me up and down with many more when we saw each other in person.

"Hey, Sheriff," she said as we were about to hang up, "you get any leads on the Hinckle kid?"

"Yeah," I assured her, "we're about to wrap it up."

She said something else, but I hung up without hearing it. I made one more phone call and then snuck out the back to go meet Tammy and Cliff.

The "safe place" is what we named the old, abandoned church tucked away in the woods about three miles behind our house, next to a nearly dried-up fishing hole called Grandpa's Pond. Grandpa referred to the scion of the Allen tribe of Central Maine, Ebeneezer Allen, who was rumored to have taken up arms and fought bitterly against first the French, then the British, and then upon arriving home a decorated patriot and veteran, he waged pitched real-estate battles against his fellow neighbors, to amass the county-wide land the family once commanded before aggressive taxation swallowed most all of it.

The old church was the original house of worship erected by Ebeneezer along with other strong folk from local farming and logging families, kept in good use for almost two hundred years before bad weather finally outpaced repairs to the roof and the town reluctantly approved and built the new house of worship in town, near Main Street. The old building was supposed to become a recreational center, but decades passed with no action. In recent years, it had become a hangout for teenagers. Under my watch, the mostly harmless young adults got a free pass until they almost set fire to the place one cold winter night. From that point, I'd kept the front and basement doors padlocked and sealed up the window spaces, whose glass was broken long ago. Now, the only ones getting inside to party were spiders and mice. The bugs and vermin are welcome to practice any faith of their choosing as long as they scatter out of sight on the rare occasions of emergency when the moldy, damp space becomes a place of refuge for the Buskin family.

A number of years ago when Cliff was still a child, a guy living about forty miles north sent a letter to every local office in the county with sheriff and deputies' home addresses and dates that he was going to blow our houses up. He turned out to be a harmless whack-job who spent six months in prison after apparently taking one holy hell of a beating upon being apprehended, but a long week of stressful days and nights passed before we arrested him. For that anxious stretch of time when I had to be out at work, instead of leaving them home alone, I unlocked the old church and set up Tammy and Cliff in a tent on the altar with a lantern and battery-powered heater and a bonus liter of Coke for the kid and bottle of wine for the wife. Since then, we've called it the "safe place" and, although keys were always kept at the ready, we've never had to use it again, until now. I supposed that if I had to break my long absence from any house of worship, then Sunday was the best day for it.

After sneaking out of the station the way I snuck in, I tried my damnedest to walk back to my truck without a limp. I wanted to appear as if it were any other afternoon and I was busy doing my job. When someone honked their car horn as I neared my ride, I simply raised a hand, not bothering to risk even the shortest chat. Sorry, can't talk now, too busy trying to close a case.

It felt good to be back in the cold but cozy truck again, and I took simple pleasure in executing a slow and careful three-point turn before motoring off at the kind of reasonable speed that would've earned the highest praise from any driving instructor. I also paused good and long at the first stop sign, sadly admiring Main Street's picturesque simplicity as the shop windows glowed in the close to setting sunshine.

I looked on toward *The Deuce*, only a few blocks down yet miles away, like the visible coast to a sailor caught in a storm's current while his vessel drifts powerlessly out to sea. From behind, somebody broke me out of my ruminations with a loud honk of their horn, so I took a right turn and left behind me way too much more than I could think about now.

The hardest part was driving past our house. It was much too early to consider selling the old place and living somewhere else, but just the thought of it not being our home anymore was terribly hard. Once word got out about the accident, we might not even be able to move it on the market. If any of the Hinckle brothers were still loose, the place was one big bullseye and reason enough to pack up and get out of town, probably hole up in a motel for a good while. Sadly, Tammy's bound for lock-up, so maybe Cliff and I can look at it like we're on a bizarre little vacation, just another father and son eating pizza and watching TV while waiting for our family's punishment to be laid down so that life can get moving again and everyone can forget what awful people we are. I never will, that's for damn sure.

Late afternoon was losing its final grip on the day when I pulled up outside the old church. The shade had entirely engulfed the building, darkening the weather-ravaged pine exterior, which shows the remnants of a hundred white paint jobs that could not hold off the decay of time, failing like a discarded temple of some long-lost tribe. The pitched timber roof was stripped bare of its last shingle, and only the steeple stood tall in defiance of age, despite its own wear and tear.

Beeping the horn three times and then waiting ten seconds before two more quick beeps was the signal to Tammy that it was her husband outside. As I climbed the creaking front steps, I called out to them.

"It's OK, guys. I'm here."

It appeared they had hurriedly unlocked and entered the church upon arrival, because the big chain was still dangling from the door handles. The strong smell of animal droppings and mold filled me up as I entered. Because there was no basement below the rotting floorboards, the whole place was damp.

Tammy and Cliff were seated by the tent heater on a couple of camp chairs we had left behind. A close race was underway between mother and son as to who looked colder and more scared.

"Hey," I said warmly, "welcome to the Lord's forgotten

outpost."

"Stop it, Blake!" Tammy warned, "It's still a holy place."

Of course, she was right, and the inside of the church was its most divine feature. With no concrete or limestone to work with in the old days, the builders had constructed the foundation with tight lines of wide standing pillars taken from massive pine trees, years later fortified with beams, braces and plaster, attaching the walls to the exterior so that the interior took on the atmosphere of a massive log cabin.

What sets it apart from many other backwoods churches erected out of crude materials and strong faith is that the early architects of Rock Hollow decorated the interior pillars by carving the stations of the cross directly into the wood. They don't stand in comparison to the fine biblical screens or frescoes of Europe, but in my hardly credible opinion the passion and energy that went into these noble works of primitive beauty equals anything created in Rome. The altar also stands as a testament to the earth, and it was fashioned from huge pieces of blue stone hauled from the surrounding woods. Like the pine pillars, smaller chiseled iconography covers the sides and surface of the thick slabs.

When I reached Tammy and Cliff, they engulfed me in hugs, and we set to crying and apologizing like a family of fish swimming in suffering and shame. Tammy appeared to be on the verge of a breakdown, but she seemed to calm somewhat as she got more off her chest about the accident.

"You were out working and…I never should've gone. He…Keith was in town and really drunk and nobody would give him a ride and it was snowing…" She cast a long shameful glance at Cliff, who never looked up. "He threatened to come to our house so…I swear, it was just to get him home. I've stayed far away ever since you…Oh God, we hit…we…*I* killed that boy and…we…drove off. And, Blake, I knew you'd kill Keith when you found out, you swore to me that you would…and then you'd be in trouble and…I'm so sorry, I just thought…if you believed Cliff did it then maybe you'd make it go away. My God! I'm so fucking awful!"

Finally, she broke down in a flurry of sobs, and although I tried to help her, she pushed me away, so I let her go on, which got Cliff started. They collapsed upon each other, and that allowed me to wrap my arms around them both.

"I just wanted to help Mumma!" Cliff wailed as he let out his own pent-up sorrow. "I had to help her. I had to!"

After they had let it out and calmed, we all broke off. Tammy shook her head and blew out an enormous sigh while mopping her face with tissues from her pocket. She then pointed at some backpacks nearby.

"I got clothes for us." She went over and picked up one of the bags. "Let's go."

I spoke slowly and deliberately, as if she were about to jump off a bridge. "Listen, we aren't going anywhere."

"What?" Cliff's eyes met mine, and he looked more exhausted than I've ever seen him. "But Mum's in trouble."

"We're all in trouble." I was tempted to dump myself into a camping chair but remained standing. "And we're going to get through it…but running ain't the answer."

"No!" Cliff exploded. "No! We've got to go!"

"Stop." I wrestled Him into a hug. Although he struggled, it seemed like he wanted to stay there.

"No," he kept repeating, "no."

"Maybe we can stay here." Tammy was crying, "At least for a little while…"

"The state cops will get here pretty soon," I confessed, letting go of Cliff.

"You…you called them…" He was surprised but not shocked, then his face grew red as he screamed, "Why can't you protect us!"

Tammy was bawling now, and she let herself drop to the altar's dusty stone floor.

"Both of you, listen to me, damn it!" I shouted, "I have been running away and lying my ass off and shooting people and getting shot at for days, and for what? For this fucking mistake, this accident!"

"It's all my fault," Tammy cried. "I shouldn't have...I should have saved that boy!"

Cliff fell to his knees and embraced her. At that moment, I could've picked up those bags and thrown both of their blubbering asses in the truck and driven for hundreds of miles. I nearly did exactly that before I was struck dumb. It was unavoidable, really, considering our present location. My eyes drifted up above Tammy and Cliff to settle on the *pièce de résistance* of offering to the divine that those first settlers had left behind. They had taken even wider pine trunks than those lining the walls and raised and mounted them behind the altar in the shape of a massive crucifix. *Well, there it is.* You can't possibly get any more guilt-inducing than Christ on the cross, even though he was crudely carved and rubbed away by time. Everybody knew who was up there.

"We're all guilty," I whispered and eased a hand onto both of their heads, staring into tormented faces. "But of what? Being scared? Protecting our family? Being human and running when something awful happens? What happened can't be changed...but we can face up to it and forgive each other at least."

"I am so sorry," Tammy whimpered.

I kneeled down with them. "Me too, but we know that boy's mother. We had her in our home, and she won't ever...We need to give her this. The awful truth is she's got to know who killed her kid so she can hate and rage and then hopefully finally just cry it all out until she picks up and keeps going. Same as us."

"He's right," Cliff said so softly that he sounded like a little kid again.

Tammy cried some more and then looked at Cliff and then me, wiping her eyes and nose on her jacket sleeve.

"I know. I know."

"We never asked for this." I gritted my teeth as if there could somehow still be a fighting way out but then went easy into the next words. "But like you said to me before, Tammy. That boy's dead, but we're alive. We've got to go on."

We all heard the distant siren mixing oddly with the outside evening chirps of those early-arriving birds that Toby had been searching for. I figured I should go out and stand on the front steps with my hands up to avoid any ugly confusion, but the phone message left earlier should've been disarming enough. I'd told the state police dispatcher where the perpetrator in the hit-and-run could be found, and that they were unarmed and atoning for their sins in a house of worship.

Not wanting to let go of this last chance to be together as a family until who knew when, we huddled on the filthy altar, saying how much we loved each other and reminding ourselves that there was forgiveness at the end but only if we earned it. The siren grew louder and eventually cut off at the sound of the vehicle skidding to a halt out front. The officers shouted warnings, and boots landed loudly on the steps outside, while I squeezed Tammy and Cliff tight.

In that moment, what held me with a suffocating grip was the shameful regret that this was as close as the three of us had been in a long, long time.

Epilogue

As far as my fucked-up family goes, the days and weeks following the arrest were the hardest on Tammy, who hadn't spent a night away from at least one of us since Cliff was born. She went through a solitary hell while Cliff and I skulked around the house imagining her suffering and bringing the same upon ourselves in our own way. As expected, word of the arrest spread like wildfire. After several hours in a cell at the station, the state police moved Tammy to a lockup about fifty miles south to await trial. Not long after that the crowds began pelting our house with rocks and similarly primitive projectiles as well as more expensive assaults with eggs. Cliff and I decided to bug out immediately, taking only the necessities. And after a few nights in a motel, we went on to tough it out over the next months in a small, rented two-room cabin on a lake further upstate. The weather wasn't great and the only heat came from a wood stove the size of a microwave oven, but the quiet did wonders for both of our nerves and allowed us to make some early, bumpy strides at patching up our relationship, even though I gave him as much space and alone time as he needed.

The lawyer we found for Tammy, a slick middle-aged ex college quarterback out of Bridgton named Jack Spade, was pretty good and he gave us a break on fees due to the case potentially boosting his career with sorely needed publicity. Spade ordered us all to plead complete ignorance about how or why the suspect vehicle had gone missing, and through his work, Cliff and I somehow escaped any criminal charges. No one outside of our family knew exactly what had gone on during that terrible weekend, and to limit the damage we pleaded the Fifth to just about everything. Luckily, none of the folks whose path that I'd crossed as the whole drama played out made any kind of incriminating statement to the authorities, including Tom Sullivan who explained to the authorities that the gas station heist was a silly mistake and ordered his employee into silence in exchange for keeping his job.

When April, that notoriously cruel month, dropped its cold, damp grip and May flew by in a rushed mix of sunshine, blooming flowers and rainstorms, Cliff and I together welcomed the first warm breaking of summer and braced ourselves for Tammy's days in court. Just as I'd hoped and Jack Spade deftly conjured, the vanished vehicle from the fatal accident resulted in a long trial and Tammy did pretty well, starting off unable to speak a word on the stand due to incessant bawling and finally coming around to explain her actions as a result of gripping fear and panic. It seemed as if everybody in the courtroom came away with the impression that this woman was certainly guilty but also appeared thoroughly regretful for her actions.

Her regret may have touched the hearts of the jury, but not so the judge, who sentenced Tammy to nine years in exchange for a guilty plea to manslaughter. Mariel Hinckle stood in the courtroom and screamed her demands for her former friend to receive the maximum punishment, and the rumor soon circulated that she swore to shoot Tammy dead on the day she stepped out of prison, vowing that her hatred would burn out of control no matter how many years she had to wait.

None of the Hinckle brothers attended the court proceedings because they were all locked up awaiting trials of their own. Big brother Ben was picked up by the state police walking back to town after his armed spectacle at the festival and before he could even be accused of robbing the gas station, he knocked one officer in the head and tried to seize the other's weapon. Apparently, Ben had outstanding weapons, assault and extortion warrants in New York and Rhode Island. Because he was on probation, once the officers had beaten him to a pulp, they transported him to the state police barracks where he remained locked up until a lawyer could be coerced into representing him.

The other two bozos got banged up pretty bad after nosediving into the landfill at the dump. The ambulance got there just in time for Derrick, who had head injuries that took a while to recover from, but just like his brothers, the prize awaiting at the end of his convalescence was a nice, long stay in prison for possessing illegal firearms while on probation for check fraud, drug dealing and, strangely, public exposure at a nursing home.

As for Dicky, he had more complaints and warrants than you could count, ranging from armed robbery to sexual assault. Because he was acting wild and out of his mind as they cut him out of the wreck, and despite busted bones and shattered teeth, they never even let him go to the emergency room. He went straight to the psychiatric hospital over in Wheaton where he was not only placed in solitary confinement but strapped to a bed for his own safety.

Lydia, as expected, was on a mission to destroy me. As she had no proof of my doing anything straight-out illegal, her only recourse would be to give me the boot and there was no way in hell that I was going to give her the satisfaction of taking my badge. The next morning after Tammy was taken into custody, I left a letter of resignation along with my town-issued handguns on the reception desk at the station and cleaned out my shit.

My next stop was one final visit to *The Deuce,* where I convinced Mickey to apply to the academy and run for sheriff in the next election. He's a nice young man who is well liked around town, and with some military service in his background, he's got a good story to tell voters. Really, anybody'd be better than the creeps that ran against me last time. While I bought Elmore a couple of stiff drinks and kicked back a root beer myself, he laid out his plan to run a small town Psyop campaign to ensure Mickey's victory in the election. At the very least, I had some guarantees that folks wouldn't bore each other to death in my absence.

It was impossible to send Cliff back to high school that spring, so he had to do lots of online summer work. By the end of August, he had earned his diploma just in time to keep his spot at the university. He's there now and enjoying the hell out of himself, solemnly promising to hit the books just as hard as the keg parties.

After all the attorney bills were paid, we had a little less than twenty thousand dollars in our family's bank account. I withdrew enough to barely cover Cliff's first year college costs and then asked the lawyer to cut a check for the rest of it to Mariel Hinckle. We still have a bunch of years left on our home mortgage, but after the eventual sale, it should get Cliff through school just fine with something extra to start out with after graduation.

As for me, I found an apartment in a town that's about halfway between Cliff's college in New Hampshire and Tammy's correctional center in Maine. The judge might have doled out a harsh sentence but he also allowed Tammy to serve most of it in a minimum-security prison, so I'm able to see her once a week for four hours. In a weird way, once we started talking through all the hurt that we'd caused ourselves and others, we rediscovered some of the things that got us hitched in the first place. She cries every time we meet, but she also winds up laughing a little and talking about stuff we'll do when she gets out. It's given me inspiration to find some steady work, because I figure you need to save twice as much for a second chance at a happy marriage.

I've also decided to never go near law enforcement again, not even a security guard job, even though they're plentiful and pay well. For short-term cash, I've been accumulating equipment and getting back into landscaping, cutting lawns, trimming hedges, raking leaves—the kind of work where you can spend all day outside by yourself. Suppose I'll have to pick up a second-hand plow for the winter and start clearing snow from driveways to make ends meet. In the meantime, I spend every daylight hour all week mowing except for Saturdays when I drive out to see Tammy, and every other Sunday when I make the ride to see Cliff and we eat Mexican food at a restaurant off campus. He says he's still having some nightmares about everything that went down, and he talks to a school health counselor regularly, but otherwise we might have gotten him back on track for a normal life.

Any Sunday that I don't ride out to see Cliff, I attend mass at a church near my new place. Not that I'm searching for forgiveness, which can only come from within, and there isn't any way I can get past killing Keith Griffin. There was clearly no choice. He would've done the same to me if his aim had been a little better. The bitter truth is that from the moment I first shot dead that armed robber in the woods, I began roaming this earth as a killer, and the deep, awful guilt had to be tucked away so I could keep going. Now, ever since I murdered Keith, I've felt like a sinner.

These days, it's only when I'm sitting on a wooden pew in church listening to the familiar cadence of the priest going through the liturgy or dolling out wry words of wisdom in his sermon that I think maybe there's a chance to get myself back somewhere close to the person I was before all the violence. The hope of a little normalcy in life is what gets me up in the morning. After long, hard hours of work, when I drop at night, exhausted and alone in my cramped apartment, other than thinking about Cliff and Tammy, I drift off to sleep hoping that, even if tomorrow won't be any different from today, at least in some little way, I can be.

FINIS

Author's Note

"A Sin to Know" began as a short story several years ago, written after a series of fatal hit-and-run accidents in our county in upstate New York. The depravity of striking someone and leaving them to die set off grief for the victims and a panicky anxiety for my own family — but also disbelief and anger at the perpetrators, which launched some burning moral questions. Those questions became the tale of a small-town sheriff whose investigation into a fatal hit-and-run lands far closer to home than he ever imagined. The next spark — the one that ignited the story into a novel — came during a family trip to Italy. I had finished the short story only a month earlier, but the moral issues it raised were still smoldering somewhere inside my head. On a long, incredible tour of the Vatican, surrounded by the immense beauty and suffering painted on the walls and ceilings, particularly in the Raphael Rooms, I realized I was using too small a boat to fish for the whale-sized answers I was seeking. It was after long, craned-neck stares at Michelangelo's *The Last Judgement* in the Sistine Chapel that everything clicked. To explore evil, Satan would have to be my starting point — not in a strictly Christian sense, although that's part of it — but through a literary lens, like John Milton's *Paradise Lost.* I knew I didn't want Satan himself as a character. Instead, the all-too-human sheriff from my short story would, over the course of the novel, endure his own fall from grace — and nowhere more deeply than in his own mind. As Milton wrote, "The mind is its own place, and in itself can make a Heaven of Hell, a Hell of Heaven."

To the families and loved ones of those lost in fatal hit-and-run accidents, you have my enduring and deepest condolences.

TPH

Other Works by Terence Patrick Hughes

Fiction
Short stories published in:

Press Pause Press
Rock Salt Journal
Portrait of New England
Egg+Frog
Review Americana

Visit:
www.TerencePatrickHughes.com

For inquiries:
media@terencepatrickhughes.com

www.ingramcontent.com/pod-product-compliance
Lightning Source LLC
Chambersburg PA
CBHW072241180726
48408CB00032B/1211

* 9 7 9 8 9 9 4 8 4 3 7 1 0 *